RESOLUTIONS

A Family in Stories

JEN KNOX

AUXmedia, a Division of Aquarius Press

Detroit, Michigan

Resolutions: A Family in Stories

Cover art: Red Ghost
Author photo: Christopher J. Shanahan

ISBN 978-1-7330898-7-6
LCCN 2020932382

AUXmedia LLC
www.AUXmedia.studio

Printed in the United States of America

This book is dedicated to Gloria.

"The phoenix must burn to emerge." — Janet Fitch

CONTENTS

JASMINE

ARCADE

Columbus, Ohio — 2016

When there's a shift I feel unsteady, like someone gave me a good shove. My pelvis aches and my forehead pulses. The physical symptoms that began twenty years ago are acute when I'm stressed, and there is nothing more stressful than being abandoned by your child.

Coming here helps. I squeeze the trigger of a plastic gun and the decades collapse into a moment. I see that younger version of myself, the day I was cursed. The trivia game that sat at the edge of the bar was my regular station then, and most of the answers were either obvious or memorized. Only the last one stumped me. It asked for the smallest country in the world. The sound of error, a brash *errrrrrr* from the computer speakers, caused the man across the bar, a regular, to raise his eyebrows.

"Thought you knew all the useless information in the world," he said. I had selected Monaco, but when I got it wrong, I learned more about Vatican City and Monaco than I would have had I guessed correctly. The clouded screen told me that there are more wealthy people per square foot in Monaco than in any other country, and this thought would occupy my mind for years.

The idea that I could stop into a coffee shop and just know that the person I'm speaking with is probably a millionaire tickles me to this day. In my neighborhood, in Ohio, there aren't many coffee shops, but if you walk into one, you're guaranteed that the person you're speaking with is *not* a millionaire.

I was thinking some such thing that day as I stared at my score. I had earned 54,000 points. JAZZ, my nickname, was already next to #1 with a perfect 60,000, so I typed MONACO in the #2 space.

"Guess that means I'm cut off," I told the regular and cringed as his chuckle turned to a gurgling cough.

"Lightweight," he said, and I forced a smile, taking my last sip of carbonated water.

I suppose you could argue that it wasn't fate but the fact that I had to pee that really led me stumbling into an old Victorian house less than a block from home that day. And you could also say that I didn't have to believe the man I met there. But you'd be wrong. It was God, in some shape or form, who led me there. And God showed up as a tiny bald man with tangy breath.

The house had a black sign out front with an eye painted on it, and when I opened the front door, I found a directory of astrologists, psychics, numerologists, and hypnotists who shared the space. "Find balance by knowing yourself," a small sign promised, so I stared at the names with narrowing eyes.

That's when he appeared, cleared his throat and told me, in lieu of saying hello, that my body gave off high frequencies of energy.

"I can provide balance, but you'll need to focus." He gestured toward an overstuffed chair in the waiting area and took a seat across from me, close enough that our knees almost touched. "Most people live at wavelengths that invite stability and contentment as they age. Not you, young lady. You'll have to decide."

"Are you saying I won't age, or I won't slow down?" I asked, realizing that I still had to pee.

He clasped his hands behind his head and leaned back, examining my Nirvana shirt with a little too much scrutiny. "You have too many spirits," he said. When I didn't respond, he continued to assess me with hooded eyes, eyes that were almost closed. He leaned in, cupping his hands around my then-young face, tracing my cheekbones as though they were marble. "Let go."

I remember the warmth that pulled up from my lower belly. I wanted to punch his face in, but everything he said felt true. My muscles released as his hands hovered above my skin. Time moved slowly, as though we were surrounded by water. He lit a candle and told me to rub oil on the heels of my feet at night for the next forty days. I felt normal, more normal than ever before, for a long time after.

But, eventually, the shifts returned, the perpetual imbalance, and I never found him again; his voice became a sentence as I walked into the same Victorian house weekly, asking after the small bald man. Spiritual posers, all of them, offered me readings or hypnosis sessions, but no answers.

"Energy like yours is volatile. Watch it closely," the bald man had told me before I left that day, and now I feel it.

When it happens now, the shifts, I sometimes go to church. I sometimes chant or find others who are supposedly as in tune as that man—none of whom tell the truth. I sometimes read facts and spend hours memorizing them to distract myself, as I did when I was a child. Or, I come here and grind my feet deep into the stained carpet on a Tuesday afternoon.

Today, I am a single mother of four, and I am full of rage. I imagine the faceless monster in front of me represents everything holding me back. I am standing wide-legged and steady, my arms straight and strong. The manageable world awaits; I know it does. I focus on it, this manageable world, and position my finger above the center of the trigger.

Humming the theme music from *Jeopardy*, I press rapidly and with all the strength I can manage, cursing my delicate hands. Weak hands from repetitive motion. They ache with the vibrations that follow each shot, the squeeze and release. The world buckles beneath me, and I exhale.

All I want is to protect her, to protect all my children. I imagine each of them an individual spirit, whole where I am fragmented. But I worry they are susceptible to the shifts. I hum louder, shooting again. My shot lands in the center of the monster's chest, and a man watching offers a slow clap. "Lucky shot," he says, jarring me from my thoughts as my points accumulate with dings and chimes.

"No such thing as luck," I say. I haven't dated anyone since Jackson, the kids' father, but this man's voice has a rasp that feels familiar. His slow smile seems rehearsed, and I stare at him for a while. I have no need to flirt, no desire. But meeting him feels convenient and inevitable; the tattoos along his arm are brilliant and clean, like a compact memoir.

He is younger than I am by at least ten years, which means he will keep up with my boys. I glance at the snake on his arm, and he smiles again. Deliberate. There is no threat, no danger of falling in love; just a

11

man to keep me company and stay out of my way.

***

Months pass and Allie is still gone. I wake to this absence. She wrote to her sister, whined about me being too controlling, too intense, promised little Molly May that she'll come back one day and get her. When I read the letters, I felt relief that she was able-bodied enough to write with such anger, but I was enraged for the exact same reason.

I wake up from a recurring nightmare that she is found dead like her father. This is how I begin my forty-second birthday. I check my phone for the local news. Three of my four children are making noise downstairs, and it's not even 7 a.m. I smell coffee and bacon, the sweetness of syrup, and pancakes with cinnamon.

After I brush my teeth, I spend a few minutes puffing out each cheek as though I can undo the wearing away. There are wrinkles left from the way I used to narrow my eyes before I knew I needed reading glasses. There is the way my mouth droops a little at the edges, and I want to destroy the mirror.

If only I could take off for good, before I'm too old.

But to be a mother is to be stuck managing a perpetual circle of safety, making sure everyone is warm and fed and in proper position. If I ran away, I'd end up on the local news with barely audible but dramatic music playing in the backdrop. The feature would be called "Mothers Who Run," and I would be there, the irresponsible mother of four.

I earned freedom, I would tell the interviewer. *I've worked harder than any damn body I know for the last two decades. I deserve this.*

I hear something break downstairs.

"Mom. We made you pancakes," Myron calls as I ease down the stairs, fastening my nametag and shaking my head. Joey picks up the pieces of a shattered plate. I was hoping they'd forget like they did last year. "You should call off work and stay with us!"

My youngest, Joey, washes his hands and presents elaborately decorated pancake faces with whipped cream beards and chocolate wire rims. He is a happy child, and I smile when I'm near him. Molly May offers a gentle glance from the table and gets up to grab a mug of coffee with milk that she has frothed on the stove. Rattle, the man whose memoir

12

has revealed itself over the last few months, cracks his neck, which sets my teeth on edge. *No danger of falling in love.*

I'm not in love, but when I ask Rattle to pray or chant, he does. When I ask him to take out the trash, I know I won't have to check out back the next morning. When I ask him to rub my shoulders after a double shift or one of my gigs, he doesn't even bat an eye—just pats the couch and gets to work. We go to the arcade together, and he helps with the bills.

The pancakes look fattening; they're drenched with syrup. "I don't have time to eat these." I reach for the coffee, winking at Molly May, who is always *just there*, as Rattle gets up from the couch with a grunt and heads toward the food.

"Hell, I'll celebrate on your behalf. Who is this supposed to be anyway?" he asks Joey, sticking his finger in the whipped cream.

"It's the hipster version of Santa. He owns his own brewery," Joey says.

"Right. Of course," Rattle says as he cuts the pancake face in two.

"Bring it in," I command, and the boys give me a hug. Molly May is close behind, and the void of Allie—though she would likely just stare at the wall instead of offering any kind of physical contact—stings. "Rattle, can you call the insurance company about credit for that security sticker out front?"

"On it."

I survey the living and dining rooms, then the small kitchen, as though she'll somehow appear with a card or a cupcake. I'd even take her fuck-you attitude. But the girl, for now, is a ghost. Like her father. She's an image that I can only bring up online.

My eldest, the version of myself that I failed to keep safe, is my crucible. Forty-two years of energy rages as I spend hours driving, looking for her. I drive both before and after long shifts.

Today a man in a sleek blue suit is walking in the middle of the street, slowing me down near the arts district downtown. He glides toward the old Victorian house, which is now a café, and I park at a meter that requires a three-dollar deposit. The man heads across the street and opens the heavy front door. He disappears into a warmly lit room bustling with caffeinated bodies, and I see my daughter there. She's wearing a white headband and a black apron. Her hair is longer, wavy, and she stands with her shoulders back the way I taught her. She seems taller.

I make a tight fist, trying to contain my energy. I hold my rage and pain, readying myself to reach for the handle but instead close my eyes. I see that silly pancake face and the longing smiles on my children's faces.

By the time I open my eyes, there is no sensation in my hand; my fingers are the color of bone, and I release my grip. As I drive home, I feel a shift, and the blood flow returns.

MOLLY MAY

DOGS

2014—Toledo, Ohio

Because I don't have any of my own, my mother is the star of all my stories. Most of them begin with noise. The scene I can't stop replaying begins with the clanging of metal, followed by a guttural yell. My older sister, Allie, and I rushed downstairs to find a charred piece of turkey bacon stuck to a pan in the sink. The gas oven was still on, and Allie reached up to turn the dial.

Our parents were in the living room, yelling about bills, and we crouched down behind the stairs to watch as Mom threw pillows, then a chair, at Dad. I stood to intervene, but fear kept me still. Mom appeared to be hitting him, when Wolf, Dad's pup, ran behind her and gripped her calf between his teeth.

She turned around, screeching like a bird of prey, which woke my brothers. Her fists pounded the dog's flesh, plunging into its ribs and neck. Everything I knew about my mother changed in that moment, and as horrified as I was, I couldn't move. Deciding it was too much to watch, Allie instructed me to go upstairs before anything else happened. We pulled at our brothers' pajama necks when they tried to slip by us to see what was going on.

Soon, everything was quiet except for an incessant ringing in my right ear. My brothers, four and six, fell back to sleep with Allie's thin arm like a safety belt over their chests. Even Allie began her soft snore after an hour, but I couldn't settle my mind. I watched the digital alarm clock turn over, minute after minute. It wasn't yet 6 a.m., and all I could do was sit on the floor with my knees pulled into my chest, until the world felt still enough to head downstairs.

Cream was still a kitten then, and she settled on Mom's lap, purring. A towel the color of blended cherries was wrapped around Mom's leg, and her hair fell in a long twist over her right shoulder. There were tears collecting at the corners of her eyes and salt trails down her cheeks, but when she noticed me, she sat up straight. Mom squared her shoulders and motioned me over with her head.

We waited that day, the way we often waited for Dad, but this time he was gone for good.

Allie was fourteen then. I'm a month away from the age she was that day, and I often think about how lucky she is to have known Dad for a few more years. He was a drummer, an artist, an all-around good guy, she often tells me, and I always say I know, but I don't know. Memories of him are like memories of a sitcom I once watched. I struggle daily to replay any of the other episodes in my mind, but all I can see is the final scene. The fear that kept me from intervening before it was too late.

**

It's 2014, a new year, and we're staying with Grandma Dee in Toledo until Mom, who spent New Year's Eve working a double, arrives to evaluate our resolutions and drive us home. Allie rinses her mug as my brothers huddle around the kitchen window, gulping hot chocolate with multicolored marshmallows.

It snowed all night, fat flakes just sticky enough to cling to the small patches of grass in Grandma's backyard. I figure we could build something small, a snow badger or an armadillo, but when Myron begs to go outside to play, Grandma Dee insists that we complete our chores. "You have to earn your keep around here," she says, ruffling my short-cropped hair, which I immediately smooth down with my palm.

Mouths chalky from marshmallow, we march to the business side of Grandma Dee's duplex. Each room on this side of the house is a funhouse mirror image of the rooms that Grandma lives in. The hardwood floors are uneven and easy to trip over. The ceilings are tinged yellow and the vents are dusty. The air bites.

Fold-out tables line the walls of the living and dining rooms. Atop them are knitted hats and scarves, old *National Geographic* and *Woman's Day* magazines, board games, and pottery from Grandma Dee's community arts classes. The items sit in rows by type and price, below pistachio-colored wallpaper that curls at the corners. Masking tape labels ask for anywhere from twenty-five cents to fifty dollars for the oddities.

The kitchen is teeming with baskets. Easter baskets, magazine baskets, decorative baskets coiled, braided, and twined. Some are small enough to fit only a hardboiled egg, and one appears large enough to hold Joey, my youngest brother, if he were to curl up like a cat. The price tag dangling from the handle asks for twenty dollars.

Grandma raises a thick finger, interrupting my thoughts. "Molly May, I'd like you to help me dust. If you do a good job, you can take your pick of anything under ten dollars." Her eyes are lighter than mine, a honey shade like Mom's, but they aren't as intense. Grandma tries to be mean but isn't deep down, even though she can seem that way. Mom is the opposite. They are not related by blood.

"I want something in the kitchen," I say, eyeing the giant basket.

Nodding, Grandma Dee smiles, her soft gray curls bouncing. She is Dad's mom. When Dad was alive, she used to call herself *Switzerland*, and she never got involved when my parents would argue, which was every time they were in the same room. Meanwhile, Mom says that Grandma Dee is passive-aggressive because she likes to buy us loud and large toys, things that disrupt and annoy. Last year, she bought my brothers a drum set.

Mom dubbed Joey and Myron's band "The Bane of My Existence." Ultimately, she broke down and sold the set on Craigslist for forty dollars, giving them twenty to spend at Toys "R" Us and putting the other twenty into what she referred to as *our freedom fund*, an account she began soon after Dad left.

"Joey and Myron, you boys go over there and make sure those baskets are in order from smallest to largest. Stack them if you can. Leave that biggest one out for Molly May," Grandma says, scratching her belly. Her shirt is fading. It says "Change We Can Believe In," and she nods when she sees me reading it.

"What if they fall?" Joey asks as he follows his brother toward the kitchen. Myron is ten now and Joey is eight and a half. They do everything together. When Myron pauses, rubbing his chin like an adult as he surveys the room, Joey examines the baskets in front of him and rubs his own chin. They're kind of cute sometimes. Kind of.

Grandma hands me a duster the same color as Cream, who is home alone and likely wondering if we'll ever come back.

"What does Allie have to do?" I know the answer.

"Allie's going to help me in the kitchen. We're going to make a pecan pie."

"I can help with that," I say. "Or help take down the tree."

"No need," Allie says in a mature voice. "You boys be sure you don't miss any baskets." Allie looks exactly like Mom, which makes it even more disturbing when they argue. And they argue all the time.

"Next time, Molly May," Grandma Dee says. "Besides, that tree stays up." She means next year, and I don't believe her until I remember what Allie told me last night. Soon, I'll be the only one old enough to help with the pies.

Once I get started, I don't mind dusting. I get every crevice; I like to make things shine. My brothers are putting baskets on their heads and pretending Toledo is a war zone, which it might be. I hear siren after siren outside my grandmother's home but am unable to determine which are fire, police, or ambulance. I hear a dog barking, but it seems far enough off.

I survey my work; the dishware and silver are gleaming. I notice that a single saucer is a hundred dollars, the most expensive thing in the room. That much money could get me to Michigan in a Lyft. I know this because Allie figured it out yesterday on her cell. The saucer, which has two fat children holding hands in a meadow on one side and a cow on the other, is hideous. On the bottom is a dark-blue script that says someone's name. Just as I place it back down, the boys' laughter turns to crying. Myron is fake crying because Joey is really crying. He fell and bumped his elbow.

"My funny bone!"

"It's fine," I say. "Pain makes you strong. You'll be like a superhero after you've had enough pain." I say it because someone said it to me once. Or maybe I heard it on a sitcom.

Joey wipes his eyes and takes in a big snotty breath. "Can I go help Allie and Grandma?"

"Ugh," Myron says. He looks at the pile of baskets, which are more mixed up than ever, and I tell him I'll take care of it.

"Walk your brother next door," I say, and I work quickly to line up the baskets by size. I'm eager to get back to the warm side of the house myself. I can already smell something sweet. As I work, I realize the dog that's barking outside sounds closer. I go to the back door to make sure that my brothers have made it safely. There's a screen door that sticks, an outside door, then another screen and an inside door. A dog is roaming around the backyard, right next to the concrete slab that Grandma Dee calls her back porch.

The dog is a mix of things, brown with reddish areas around the ears and chest. It has a white patch on its tail that rises like a flame, and I'm not sure whether the fact that it's wagging means he wants to play or eat me. I think about Cream, her delicate movements. Mom loves cats, always has. Dogs, with their jerky aggressiveness, are to be feared. They cause rifts, sever human relationships, make fathers disappear.

The pup cannot see me, I realize. It's wagging its tail because it sees a bone that Grandma Dee must have thrown out back. The bone is near the door, and the dog is heading this way, until a squirrel runs by, capturing its attention. Grandma Dee feeds all walks of city-bound nature. The squirrels in her backyard look like furry tanks because she tosses them an entire batch of oatmeal cookies every Sunday.

***

My father's dog died with him. They had been walking early in the morning, before my father's time-and-a-half shift as a stocker at a megastore, and a drunk driver hadn't seen them. Dad never wore reflective vests like the joggers in our neighborhood. He was wearing a black hoodie when they found him on Christmas. "He must've looked like a criminal," Mom had said. She identified the body and refused to bury Dad's best friend with him, even though she knew that's what Dad would've wanted.

"Jackson is returning to spirit. That dog isn't going to be anywhere near him," she said.

The dog I watch is running toward a tree now and makes a few sloppy steps up before scrambling back down. It jumps awkwardly, wanting to catch an overweight, bushy-tailed squirrel that I'm surprised wasn't already caught. It's a scruffy dog, and I wonder if it has a home. I don't see a collar. I open the inner screen door and place my hand on the gold knob to open the outside door. I am peering out through a small glass window, and the dog looks my way.

I envision Mom's leg meat pierced. The bared teeth only disappeared with my father's command. I envision the same dog cowering as she pummeled it; the dog looking to my father for permission to retaliate. I'm sure she crippled that dog, and at the time, I thought she had killed it.

Last night, Allie told me she will soon run away from home, away from Mom. "I can't handle her intolerance, Molly. She's toxic. I'll only stay if you ask me to."

I opened my mouth, ready to ask her to stay, to beg her, but the way her jaw tensed and her eyes pleaded, it would have been selfish to ask her to stay just for me. We'd been sleeping at the odd angles that Grandma Dee's fold-out couch demanded and with our faces close enough that I could feel the warmth of her breath. "I have your permission?" she asked again and again, and all I could do was nod.

The double doors on the other side strike me as inconvenient and ill-designed. Grandma Dee is just inside that other door, but sometimes my brothers lock it from habit, so I might need to knock. If the dog attacks me, it will have ample time to bite, and the backs of my legs will be facing its teeth. My father is not here to tell it to back off. It will see my mother in me and know I am the enemy.

A tough Midwestern breeze hits, and I open the door. The dog is unimpressed, and instead of charging, it sits, watching me with a tilted head. I haven't been this close to a dog in years. Whenever Mom sees one, we give it a wide berth or try to scare it off. I squint, edging toward the door, and reach for the handle next. Two doors to go. This door could be easily knocked down. A strong wind would be all it'd take.

The dog whimpers, as though asking me something, and I turn to see its tail thumping. I am closer to its bone than it is. I could bend down and pick it up, toss it the dog's way. Sirens sound, and both the dog and I look off toward the alley.

Mom will arrive any minute. If she pulled up now, I have no doubt she'd grab the handgun she keeps in her glove compartment. She got the gun the day after Dad left, and announced it as a new presence, "the new

22

man in the house." She pulls it out on occasion, when she gets worked up about things.

I swallow and take a step, crouching down and slowly reaching for the bone. The dog wags its tail again, stands. My heart swells. When the dog stares at me, I get a glimpse, a real-life glimpse, of the past. A warmth expands to fill my ribs. The bone is dry and splintered, a small turkey bone likely left over from Christmas. I almost toss it, but instead hold it out. For some reason, I want to see the dog up close. Slowly, it edges toward me. Its tail stops wagging when someone inside, likely my stupid brother, bangs something.

"Hey, Lucky! Hey, Molly May, that's Lucky. He's harmless," Grandma yells from the kitchen window. I look up and see her slight smile. Grandma is always smiling, even though her lips never tilt up the slightest bit. "Better hurry up, though. Your ma will be here soon."

I toss the bone, and Lucky snatches it up, exposing teeth that could tear flesh. But instead of running away, he stares for a long time, examining me as though I were a puzzle. He seems familiar in a way, and I wonder if I can pet him. I take a step forward, concentrate on those gold-rimmed hazel eyes, and reach out my hand. Just as I am about to pet him, something rustles behind the house, and Lucky bounds off to chase another squirrel.

Mom never let me close to Dad's German shepherd. She made it stay out back, where Dad would sit for hours with his computer. He bought the dog sweaters in the winter, and we were only allowed near Wolf the few times Mom wasn't around. It feels like a lifetime ago, another me, but I can now remember the feeling of his fur against my small hand.

The doorknob opens easily, and I am smiling as though I just saw an old friend. I don't tell my siblings about the dog because I don't want the subject to come up later with Mom. I look out the window every few minutes, though, just to see if Lucky will come back. Grandma Dee asks me to help her with the dishes. And, when Grandma and I are alone later, I whisper that she should feed Lucky more bones. I offer to let her keep the giant basket and get him more bones when she sells it.

***

When Mom arrives, she's in a sleek brown coat with faux fur around the hood. It's new, either from the thrift store or her boyfriend, because Mom never spends money. Not long after she arrives, we are all around the kitchen table, heads down, pens in hand.

Grandma has put on a cardigan over her shirt, but I can still make out the edge of the letters. I too want change. I click my pen. My brothers are unfocused, so I help them with their resolutions.

Allie calls Mom a Resolution Nazi. Mom likes to say that we're a goal-driven family on an upward trajectory. "We're go-getters, and go-getters make SMART goals," she says, looking over our shoulders like the worst kind of teacher.

She smells like sweat and drugstore perfume today, which I try to ignore. My actual resolutions are a different story. I want to own a dog one day. I want to live with my sister in an apartment in the city, develop a taste for coffee.

Mom takes small bites of her pie. "You should sell these," she tells Grandma Dee. It's a moment between them, something soft. Grandma's baking can soften the most stubborn of souls, which is why she earns so much on rummage-sale days. People come for the free pie and buy her junk to justify seconds, even thirds. As soon as Mom's plate is clean, it's back to business. The house smells like ginger and cloves; we watch as Grandma's neighbor's house is dusted with more snow. The roads will be slick.

Mom reviews our resolutions with a red Sharpie. "Allie, come on. If we want to change our lives, we need to think big," she says, balling up the paper and tossing it into the tall white trash can across the room.

"Why not just write them for us, then?" my sister asks. Mom flicks her dead center of the forehead, and I see a red welt begin to form.

"Don't talk back."

I glance over at the trash can. I want to know what my sister wrote, but just as I stand to sneak the paper out, Grandma scrapes the remains of Mom's pie crust into the same trash can. Allie's rage is funneled into her pen. She presses hard into the paper. She looks to me, and I look away. The room is silent for minutes, then come the clanging of dishes and shifting of papers. I feel Mom's breath on my ear as she bends over my list.

She is looking for specificity. I never know what to write, but I do

24

know what to avoid, and so I write what she'll want to see. I will soon be a faster runner, like Allie, and able to run a full mile. I will get a perfect report card. I will be kind to my brothers and not put Joey in the giant basket and leave him on someone's door because he's been crying too much. I scratch that one out, but Mom can still read it.

"Add timelines. Goals should be time-bound. And what does this one mean? A giant basket." Her fingernail traces #7.

"Ah, the basket!" Grandma Dee claps her hands and goes to retrieve my prize. "I'll load the kids' haul in the truck," she says. "Would you like me to wrap up some food for you to take home, Jasmine?"

Mom shakes her head, looking severe. I notice the swelling around her eyes and wonder if I'll ever be so tired. "Hold on just a minute," she says when she sees Grandma with the oversized basket. "You meant that one literally, eh?" she asks me.

"Yeah, hold on a minute," I say. "I want the basket money to go to Lucky."

Ordinarily, I do everything I'm supposed to do. I don't say a word, but something inside of me is alive now. I have a second heartbeat and another set of lungs. I close my eyes and see my father, the brown boots he wore with jeans, shuffling back and forth as he tried to keep a squeaky plush toy away from Wolf.

We head to the truck, my brothers cramming into the back of Mom's '90 Ford with droopy faces and over-sugared brains, when I see Lucky again. I want to run after him. Mom is telling us about her drive and how she almost ran out of gas and never realized how few stations there were along the way. She says this should be a lesson to us.

"I got you all gifts. Thank you for slumming it with Grandma Dee," she says. When she says "slumming it," I clear my throat.

My sister's body tenses. I hear her thoughts. I know she wants to tell Mom how wrong she is about everything: about dogs, my father, and especially about Grandma Dee. I see my sister's lips part when I blurt out, "We weren't slumming it. Don't—" I look to my sister. "Don't talk about her that way." My voice is shaky, but the words solidify in the air.

Allie nods her assent as Mom's eyes glaze over us from the rearview mirror, narrowing; just as I expect retaliation, another truck cuts her off.

Mom releases her hands from the steering wheel. "What the hell is wrong with you?" she yells, sticking her head out the window. My brothers join in.

"Yeah, man! What the hell?" Myron yells. Joey laughs. Mom revs the car, tailing the truck, which is twice the size of her Ford, before returning to the speed limit.

"Watch yourself, Molly May," she says at last.

"She can say what she wants," Allie says. She and Mom catch eyes in the rearview, and this is when I know that there's no changing my sister's mind. I grab Allie's hand as we ride home, thinking about what she told me last night.

There is a certain magic that Allie and I share, and it allows not only thoughts but entire philosophies to be communicated between us without a single word. A part of me wants to tell her to stay, or to bring me with her when she leaves home, but the bigger part knows better. Instead, I make it a point to remember everything while my sister is around. Allie's hand is cold and strong; she rests her head in the crook of my neck and I smell her apple shampoo. We keep our eyes on the road, knowing that this silence will only last so long.

Together, we look for novelty and find it everywhere. We see it sparkle in the snow, in the footprints near fences, and along the narrow emergency lanes of the road. I wonder what it'll be like to take a right turn just because, to make the decision to be kind. Right now, I imagine this ride could last forever.

LOST HER WAY

Columbus, Ohio—2016

Without Allie, the world is hushed. Even when my brothers roar like lions, Mom stomps around on clunky heels before work, or Rattle—Mom's new house-arrest boyfriend—gets restless and plays Norwegian Metal at decibels that could split an eardrum, I don't hear much. Everything is static without my sister.

I wonder what Allie would say about Mom's new gig as a part-time beauty consultant/model, or the single job she landed last August. I had to babysit my brothers last week as Mom spent hours posing in a skin-colored bathing suit, arms akimbo, in front of a green screen.

Allie would've gone with her had she been around; she would've read and reread the small print on the contract. Instead, Mom came back with three hundred dollars in crisp bills that would go into her savings and a Xerox copy of the agreement that would act as little more than proof that she had signed away rights to her image, and any manipulation thereof, in perpetuity.

Customers of Lee's Mature Fashions can now view my mother, at 360 degrees, wearing any of the company's outfits. Not only can customers dress and undress her to that nude bathing suit, they can also widen or stretch parts of her body to better replicate their own hips or height. Mom almost broke her laptop when she saw herself in a flower-print dress she couldn't afford, her breasts plumped and her cheekbones severe to offset the innocent print.

Since Allie ran away, Mom's dreams have become erratic. She reads self-help books that tell her she can manifest anything, and she believes she is entitled to do just that. But I'm not sure she knows what she wants. There are dream boards in her bedroom, and on the fridge, drawings of a huge house with a pool, but the images are always morphing based on the latest HGTV episode.

After she picked up an extra shift at Arcade, a regular customer who *knew a guy* suggested she try mature modeling. He told Mom she could make a day's worth of tips in a few hours. She spoke endlessly about how these extra shifts and gigs would get her to her goal. She's three hundred closer, I guess, but at what cost? Exhausted people don't make time to read the small print, but they always have time to dream.

Truth is, I don't think of things like reading the small print until it's too late, but I realize my responsibility. As much as they used to fight, my sister looked out for Mom by challenging her, and when things didn't go well, she solved problems that Mom's tired but resolute decisions would make. Allie had a soothing way about her, a constant song in her voice. Mom was stronger in her presence, if only as an opposing force.

I used to imagine that Allie would one day come home for good, or at least reach out and tell me what to do. My powerhouse sister, clapping her hands and radiating laughter, the way she used to, would heal all wounds. It would probably overwhelm her to see my brothers now, how tall Joey got this year. She'd squeeze Myron's plump cheeks and make fun of my skinny legs.

The day she left, Allie promised me she wasn't leaving for good. "I'll come back for you when you're old enough. We'll take over the world together, kiddo, you and me."

That day, she asked me to hand her a book, a bra, but I just stared dumbly at the wall, unable to help her pack. Instead, I numbly stroked the soft mass of fur in my lap. Cream purred loudly, warming my legs, as Allie traced a circle on my back with her fingertips and leaned in, resting her forehead against mine. "I mean it, Molly May. In the meantime, be strong. This shit's limiting." She tilted her palm up and made a sweeping motion around the room that signified everything; our home, our community, our reality. My reality.

Allie left notebooks filled with poems and cartoon "sheroes," a term she didn't love but had to accept when she found out that "She-Ra" had already been taken. She drew *me* as a shero. Me, with square shoulders and a determined brow, lifting my hands toward the sky. It was an image that I tore up when she left, but as the paper split unevenly between my hands, the drawing etched itself into my memory.

Allie probably reads late into the night in her small, swanky apartment now, and there's most likely a soundtrack threading through her teal headphones as she rides public transportation with the detached cool that comes with independence. I never imagined she could be right around the corner; my sister, so absent, a stone's throw away. What I found out recently is that, in her own way, she's still watching out for me.

I gave her my permission to leave because she had been suffocating. She needed to find herself, to get away. I never worried about her, not even as Mom listed all the depraved and violent things that people, especially men, are capable of when in the presence of an underage young woman.

Mom didn't sleep for weeks after Allie left. My brothers acted out, more than usual, and she just let them. A few days after Allie ran away, Myron burned his thumb on the oven and had to go to the emergency room. Joey sashayed around the living room in Mom's bikini, until she caught him and merely shrugged. She would either pray or burn sage, depending on the book she was reading at the time.

Nights, I would curl up next to Mom, reminding her of Allie's strength. I wished I could summon my sister's voice those days, hum something in tune at least, but all I could do was be there. We sat and waited for my sister to return, the same way we had waited for Dad. Shoulders square. Terrified.

"Tell me she's fine. Tell me she's not like your father."

"She's not like him, Mom," I said, because I knew that this was the reassurance that Mom needed to hear and because I had no other words. But every time I said it, another piece of me shattered.

***

In prison, Rattle tells us, there's a code for everything. Letters are *kites*, and the treasured correspondence comes from outside prison walls, otherwise known as The Free. I often feel as though I'm the one locked up, forced to go along with whatever Mom says. Allie lives in The Free. My sister, always unafraid to plant her feet, can do and say as she pleases. I imagine myself in her shoes, out there in the world, but I know I'm not ready.

My bedroom window faces a gravel parking lot. The spewing of tiny rocks from under tires at all hours used to keep me up at night. The nearest building is a pizza place with a neon sign that changes regularly. It was Pizza Cottage, Casa de Pizza, Jimbo's, Pizza Plate, and now High St. Pizza. The owners are the same, but the store is often closed after inspections and reopened under different names or with a new look, as though people won't notice and the Yelp reviews won't carry over.

The delivery people carry bright red warmers, and customers tote brown bags with expanding grease stains. I'm waiting to see my sister's face. I hope I recognize her, the shape of her, the upright posture and long neck. Allie reached out last week by way of a letter (a kite) handed to me by a kid at school I'd never seen before. The note said, simply, "Meet me behind the pizza place at 2 a.m. on February 3rd."

I recognized her handwriting, and immediately the world felt alive again. I read the note dozens of times on the bus ride home, careful to thoroughly destroy it by ripping it to shreds, then pouring water over the paper before balling the wad up and aiming it toward a dumpster. It was all very top secret. I felt like I was that drawing my sister had sketched, my arms in the air, ready to take flight after whatever came next.

Today is February 3rd. I'm passing the time by reading *1984*. Everyone at school is reading it, even though it hasn't been assigned. Unassigned books are delicious things, and since the world has been muted, at least for me, reading has become more immersing. I glance out the window after every few sentences, feeling like Big Brother could be watching. My mother, that is, could be watching. I eye the door, expecting to see her shiny hair and accusatory eyes. I survey all surfaces and corners. I wouldn't put it past her to plant a surveillance camera in my room.

It's 1:52 a.m. My window is cracked and the air is chilly. Rattle's habit of falling asleep on the couch makes it tough to sneak out the front door — something Allie couldn't know — so I'll have to crawl out the window and shimmy down the tree. My brothers do it all the time, or used to, until Mom took a broom handle to their butts. I'm confident I can do it, too.

When I push the window up another foot, it makes a loud, sweeping sound. I wait a minute, to be sure no one hears, then I fold at the waist, stepping one foot out onto the side ledge, and I duck my head. My back scrapes against the window as I step out. I assess the tree. Its oak branches are generous, like arms reaching out to embrace me.

"Get me to my sister," I tell it, and it acquiesces, at first. I hold on to one thick branch and crawl on all fours along another. It's just wide enough that my knees kiss. I remember watching Myron jump onto this tree trunk like a cat. I've never been the daredevil he is, the acrobat my youngest brother, Joey, has become. But today, I have no choice.

The wind is fierce. It slams into me like a linebacker. I wish I wasn't so skinny. Losing balance, I reach frantically for stability; my nails dig into the wood when I make contact. I will not fall, but I can feel the shudder of fear work through me. I begin to ease down the trunk, looking out over the fence toward the parking lot. I have no idea whether a few minutes or a few seconds have passed. All I know is that I still don't see my sister.

I feel secure, until I realize I'm not. I slip. My palms scrape against bark as my butt skids down, and I land on all fours, my hands and knees burning. It is here that I realize I'm going to have to climb back up at some point.

I can hear the wind and the soft sound of voices. The pizza place stays open till 2:30 a.m. to cater to those leaving the bars on High Street. The bars are starting to make last calls, and zombie-like crowds of drunkards roam the streets. My sister must have picked this time because she knows the hustle, the noise, will be a distraction.

"You have no idea what I've been through here, what you left me to go through," I want to tell her. I want to tell her about all of Mom's antics and illogical rules, how she's been coming home late and waking up angry. I think about all I am going to say as I stand next to a dumpster and nod at the occasional person who wanders in or out the back door.

I can see inside the pizza kitchen and beyond to the dining room. The place is set up with pews, like a church, and people bring their own cans of beer. Sometimes this restaurant hosts bands that play the kind of music Rattle likes. It is where he used to take Mom when Mom and he were first dating, but now he rarely leaves the couch for any reason other than to work at the gas station down the street. It has something to do with his house-arrest restrictions, though this would be within his limits.

Two guys who look like college students, in hoodies with team logos and jeans tucked into boots, come out the back and immediately squawk like birds. At first I figure they're just amusing themselves, but then I see her at the end of their gaze.

My sister, secret detective-like in all black and with her hair in a severe bun, has lips the color of cherries and dark lines exaggerating her eyes. It's an older look, a look that makes her appear eerily like Mom—when Mom was a Madonna-obsessed teenager. I feel my cheeks lifting as if they haven't in two years.

"Children, children," she says to them. She's at least a few years younger than them, and her deep tone catches them off-guard. One guy puts his hands up in a cease-and-desist motion.

As Allie stares at me through honey-colored eyes, I remember our connection—the way we can read each other's thoughts without speaking. I feel everything she wants to say before she runs my way, capturing me in a tight hug. Her grip is firm, and I struggle to release my arms so that I can hug her back just as hard. We stay like that for minutes.

"You didn't hear me calling to you, my beautiful sister?" she asks, looking me over with a smile. "Look at you! I called your name like six times and you didn't budge."

"I miss you more than I thought I would," I say, loudly.

"Me too. How's Grandma Dee?" She squeezes my hand hard.

"Good. Strong. Mom still lets us see her for the holidays."

"Who's that guy I heard in the background? He sounds like an ass."

"Rattle. He doesn't do much. Has an ankle bracelet."

"For what?"

"Aggravated assault."

"You're living with that mess? A man named after a snake. What the hell is wrong with Mom?"

I smile, reassuring my sister. "He's a tree stump. I don't think he could do anything to us. He acts like he's hypnotized most of the time."

My sister begins to pace in short form. She looks at me the way a CEO looks at balance sheets, and says, "I'll figure something out." My sister's tone is businesslike, and I imagine her structuring one of Mom's SMART goals in her head. We're trying to cover a lot of ground in a short amount of time, and I wonder if Allie has somewhere to be. She stops walking and looks at me. "Listen. I'm getting you out of there. Soon. I just need a better place. What about the boys?"

"Crazy, just like before. Really crazy. And bigger. They fall harder."

Her intensity breaks, and I squeeze her hand as she smiles wistfully. "What about you?" I ask.

She scratches the back of her neck to stall a moment, then says something I can't hear. When I ask her to repeat, she gets close to my face and says, "It's not as easy as I thought. I'm working on it. There are a lot of people interested in social justice, but not as many who show up. They don't realize that if we keep allowing those in power to pick and choose who gets right, there won't be any for any of us. You know what I mean? You do."

I don't say it aloud, but I lock her eyes and try to tell her she's strong. The clicking and scraping of nails against blacktop startles us. We watch a dog run in spurts around to the back of a corner store, and I think about Lucky. It sniffs around an upturned milk crate, sprinting and checking everything out; it's our neighbor's dog, and I remember how terrified I once was of his silly underbite. We lunge toward it from the side so that it runs home. We orchestrate this without thinking.

Allie says she'd better go. "I just wanted to check in," she says, but before she can rush off, a car with its brights on turns the corner and stops right in front of us. Like deer, we are stunned.

Mom comes barreling toward us, leaving the passenger's seat door of a pumpkin-colored Rubicon wide open. She grabs my sister by the sleeve, jerking her tenderly, like a dog picking up her pup by the neck. I notice that the car looks brand-new and has Michigan plates. I close the door. All I can do is listen, and I barely hear Allie. Mom, however, is loud and clear.

"Thank you, God! You can't do this, Allie. You can't keep doing this. We need to talk." There are tears in my mother's voice, and I wonder what she means by "keep doing this." Had my sister tried to reach me before? Allie resists, slapping Mom's hand away, and I shield my eyes from the light as I make my way around the front of the car to see who's driving. It's not Rattle; it's an older man with long hair. A guy who smiles at me as he turns off the headlights.

"Thanks for that. This is a rental," he calls out casually, as my sister and mother scream at each other. Their voices ring in my ears a moment, but then everything goes silent, and I walk around the Jeep.

"I'm Molly May," I tell the man.

"Molly May, I know. Your mother told me about you, said you help her out at her church sometimes. I'm Blake."

"Nice car."

"Thanks. Rental." We both watch Mom and Allie. "Are you used to this? You don't seem rattled." I smile at his word choice, then shrug.

"How do you know Mom?"

"The restaurant your mother works at hosted an event. I offered to give her a ride before I head home, since she worked so late to clean up. You wouldn't believe how much money we raised for cancer research, thanks to her efforts at the restaurant. Your mother could be a doctor, the hours she works."

"Ah, yeah, Mom's a saint," I say. I can't think of anything else to say. What I want to say to this man is that I will likely get my ass kicked, mentally, for days now. And I don't need the abuse.

"Looks like she's a goner." He motions to my sister, who is running at track-star speeds toward High Street. Mom stumbles after her in her work heels. "Kids are tough, eh?"

I just stare at Blake, confused as to why he felt compelled to say that to me. "Parents can be tough, too."

"You're wrong, Jasmine," my sister yells at Mom. "You are so wrong, and I hope you realize it one day."

"You'll see how hard it is, kiddo!" Mom yells back. She whips her head around and gives me a fierce look. "I'll meet you at the front door." My neck tingles as Mom gets back in the car, and they take the long way around the block. Blake nods toward me.

"Good to meet you, kid."

"Thanks. You too!" I cut through the gravel lot, and when I get to the front stoop, I crouch down and wait, barely able to hear our neighbor's dog barking. Mom and Blake stay in the Jeep a long time, long enough for me to decide that I could live in one of those cars. She emerges looking far more composed and shakes her head when she sees me crouched down as though I could blend in with my shadow. "How long have you two been sneaking around like this?" she asks. "Molly May?"

When I assure her that it was just today—the first time—she seems to believe me. "I tried to get her to come back," I lie.

She stares at me a long time. "Look, don't tell Rattle about this guy driving me home, got it? I had a sort of late night at work, and you know how he doesn't understand things."

"10-4." I look out beyond the gravel lot, and as I watch Blake drive off, I bite my lip hard enough that it begins to bleed.

Bye, Sis. My shero.

Mom and I take soft steps inside, and Rattle doesn't budge. I see his eyelids flutter. He gasps for breath between snores, but he always does this; Mom releases a sigh as she removes her jacket and heels.

"Try not to wake the boys," she tells me, and I nod.

***

The air is getting cooler and the sky is a flat Ohio gray. I glance out my bedroom window and watch the people outside; the roamers, the drunkards, the mysterious. I watch as people begin to leave without pizza boxes. I watch for my sister, hoping she'll reappear and wave, just to let me know she's doing okay. Mom interrupted us before I could find out where she is living or how I can contact her, but I gathered enough to know she's still in the neighborhood, maybe even around the way.

I'm about the age my sister was when she left home. I'm almost ready to find my way, but as I crouch down next to my bedroom window, settling in with my book, I hear Mom pacing, and I wonder if, at least for now, I can do good here. The world is quiet as I curl up in Mom's bed. She sits next to me, and we don't argue. I tell her that Allie will be fine. I tell her that Allie will be better than fine. I see the fear, a yellow tinge in Mom's eyes.

"Why'd she leave me?" she asks.

"She left us," I say.

I match the slow cadence of her breath. We can't read each other's minds like Allie and I can; Mom's ever-changing beliefs have no room in my head. But my mother is breakable beside me right now, and in this moment, I am solid, unafraid.

10-4

Columbus, Ohio—2017

If I become a cop, Rattle will be my first arrest. I don't dislike the guy, but it'll be easy, make me look tough out of the gate. The first arrest is a big deal, and I happen to know that Rattle will break the law any given day he finds breath in his lungs.

His voice is muffled through the wall. Rattle and Mom have been arguing for hours. If they don't stop fighting soon, we'll miss church service. Mom is now religious because Rattle was raised that way, which piqued her interest. Now that she has "found the light," she says, we all need to. Her gaze is determined during sermons, and sometimes, just for a moment, it's peaceful.

I'm not a huge fan of Mom's newly zealous dedication to the church, but I know it won't last. Nothing does. In the meantime, unloading my woes in song and prayer, in exchange for a well-phrased directive, feels a lot healthier than bemoaning the world and feeling bad later. I'd like to confess to Mom's God just how little I'm looking forward to the rest of the day. That's a horrible thing to say on Service Day, but all I can think about is how excruciatingly long it will be, especially with Mom in a bad mood. She hasn't made the lemon bars she promised to make. The boys aren't dressed for church, and I'm sure I'll be the one to blame for all of that.

The bass of Rattle's voice rises, and I hear him ask who Blake is. Mom's voice is louder, shrill and determined, and I only catch the occasional phrase. "If you *really* loved me, you'd," "Oh, just shut up," and "I don't need to listen to *you* telling *me* who I can contact ... I ask you to do one thing for me, and you can't..." Door slam, door slam. It's like a soundtrack.

I don't worry about Mom and Rattle fighting, but I do monitor. Mom never gets as heated with Rattle as she did with my father. I sometimes dream of my younger self stepping between my parents and placing my small, soft palms up, signaling *stop*. In the dream, they do.

The yelling picks up again, but my brothers are oblivious to the yelling. Joey is wearing Mom's floppy hat and sunglasses with his suit pants; he's taking wide, shaky steps around the bedroom and screaming, "Watch out, man! Bats!" because Rattle let him watch *Fear and Loathing in Las Vegas* last night. He's almost ten now. Myron's twelve. I'm just a few years shy of old enough to move out—that's really all age means to me. *Mom's new God: I am impatient about everything, and I'm becoming less patient with every passing day.*

I have a math test Monday and should be studying with this bit of free time. Algebra is my nemesis. It's one of the last hurdles before graduation. Once that diploma is in my hand, I can start to make moves. Major in criminal justice, or just apply to the Academy. I read blogs by female cops who warn of the perils of the job, having to prove yourself again and again, having to accept that some people will always see you as weak, no matter how strong you are. The narratives suggest I don't have a choice.

My brother smashes into the wall. "Where'd that come from? All these bats?" he asks me, wide-eyed and wavering. I rush over to him and pluck the hat off his head.

"They stole your hat," I say. I wave it around in the air slowly, as though it were between two bats, held captive in their claws. He plays along, looking up, stumbling back.

"Call my lawyer," my brother says. Joey is a theatrical kid—he acts out whatever movies he likes, and he's good at impersonations. Occasionally, Mom has someone over, and she asks him to do his ten-year-old kid's impression of Don Vito Corleone from *The Godfather*, a movie series we all saw at ridiculously young ages. When it comes to real people, Joey's especially good at imitating Rattle, his gravelly tone and nonchalance, but Rattle doesn't like it. People often have different versions of themselves in their own heads.

Joey does impressions of Myron, me, Mom, and even Allie, though he can't pretend to be her without upsetting everyone or starting an argument. The impression he does of me is overly simplistic. He'll start by looking out the window, dreamy-eyed, then say something deadpan and strange, like, "The squirrels got to the nuts after all. So much for my life's work."

Joey continues to stumble around the room as I hear a "fuck you" in baritone. I rush back to the wall. Rattle doesn't usually resort to cursing, which piques my interest. My brother appears oblivious. After pressing my ear to the wall again, it doesn't take long to get the gist. He wants to head to Vegas, win a bunch of money, and buy a new Harley.

Rattle's been on probation, or house arrest, for most of the time I've known him. He has a way of getting arrested immediately after earning full rights as a citizen, almost as though the police just know to tail him his first night off probation (my very plan) and wait for him to pick a fight with a guy at a bar or drunkenly take a piss on someone's Mercedes. The petty crimes add up, but overpopulated prisons allow Rattle to do his time at home. He's been free and clear of his last incident for almost a full 24 hours now, and he wants to go on a trip. Mom's opposed.

The air conditioning makes the wall vibrate against my ear, and I press harder, even though that doesn't make a difference. I hear him use the word "innocent" in reference to his trip. He gambles with some buddies (explains *Fear and Loathing*) and comes back ... What's the problem? What's the big deal? To Mom, this plan is catastrophic.

"Why are you standing by the wall?" Joey asks.

"To hear what's going on," I say.

"I can hear it all; hear it all, all the time," Joey says. "Maybe the bats stole your ears."

"Shhhh," I say. I listen. Everything is too muffled now.

"I love you, and I want you around all the time," Mom said yesterday, as she fingered the stem of her martini glass. Mom drinks everything out of dollar-store martini glasses lately. They break in the dishwasher, but she loves them and continues to buy them. The wide-brimmed glasses hold her apple juice, iced coffee, water—pretty much anything but a martini. She thinks the glasses evoke a sense of sophistication, like big sunglasses or a stylish outfit. She does what she can to create her own glamour here in Middle America.

No way we'll make Service Day. Just as I am about to plop back down on my bed with my laptop, Myron rushes in and tackles Joey, pinning him on the ground in a wrestling move. The boys' legs twist around like licorice, and I hear someone's pants rip.

"I'm going to *murder* in our next meet," Myron says proudly. "Won't I?" Myron looks to me with his deep-set eyes and chubby face.

"Get off him," I say.

"Yeah, fuckwad," Joey cries.

"Hey! Language. Myron, get off him. Check your pants. I heard something rip." I stand, ready to do my best to pull my chunklet of a brother off the tinier one. "If your opponent is the size of Joey, you aren't that good a wrestler. You know that, right?"

Myron rolls his eyes and walks out. I feel bad for the kid. I don't feel the bond with him that I do with Joey or did with Allie. He seems to inhabit a different planet. Bad to say, I know, but it's true. There's something missing in his eyes.

***

The truth keeps barreling at us, Molly May. You can't avoid the bad stuff, but you can fight it, slow it down, give it less of a stage, my sister wrote to me a few weeks ago. She's been leaving me notes in the tree in our backyard, top secret-like. When I'm not at school, I basically live next to my bedroom window, waiting to catch her in the act, but she's a pro. She tells me about the protests she's been involved in and why. She tells me to resist. Her last letter was relatively short:

MM: Today has been pivotal in the resistance movement. Not only did we recruit more than six hundred people with our online petition, but we also pulled off another successful protest. Are you on our mailing list?

We charged ahead on the Statehouse lawn, faced down counter-protesters with grace. One of them pushed William in the chest. I grabbed his hand and squeezed as hard as I could, feeling the heat from his skin. This guy—I know you haven't met him, but MM, let me tell you—he's no wilting flower. This guy is ex-Marines, and he once told me that his ability to disconnect from reality when he's upset, along with his reaction time, frightens him. He's usually nowhere near the frontline because he seems the kind who would incite a riot, the one who would push back. MM, he didn't. He found that strength—that thing THE OPPRESSORS don't have.

I'll come back for you soon. xoxoxo A

My sister is a leader of what she calls a radical peace movement. She says that they are peaceful warriors because their words will destroy hate. She truly has become a shero. But in one letter, after a tough night in which half her crew was arrested, she said that she is beginning to think the resistance movement should be armed, which kept me up worrying. *It might be what it takes.*

Mom says she's a fool, but I see through her anger. Rattle says he'd like to meet her and have a chat. Rattle lost his job at a factory, probably due to his last arrest, but he doesn't hold the same views as Mom. He couldn't care less about social issues, he says, but he clings hard to a special hatred for CEOs and other rich people who steamroll the poor. "They just went from exploiting us to exploiting others. Fuck 'em."

Disdain for authority is what makes Rattle a chronic offender. If he feels he's been talked down to, he starts a fight. If someone who looks like he has money gives him the wrong sideways glance, he starts a fight. If someone starts talking about traveling the world for fun, he will most definitely start a fight. Anyone who struggles, though—"That guy's okay."

In fact, those who struggle are better than okay. If you're hungry, Rattle will give you his last forkful of food, or drape his sweatshirt around your shoulders if you're cold. I've seen him stop eating mid-breakfast at Bob Evans, so he can get his food packaged up to take out to the guy who stands near 5th and Olentangy. I'd arrest him anyway.

***

Mom stands over me. She hollers, "You hear me?" I glance up, nodding my head back and forth.

"I didn't … I was just waiting here. I didn't want to interrupt."

"I've been calling you for ten minutes. I need you to move your ass. You're going to make us late to church."

I think quickly. "Can I stay home? My stomach hurts," I lie, figuring I can confess when we go later this week.

"With God in your heart, the pain will fade," she says sternly, lifting my chin. "How do you think I have it in me to work such long shifts, eh? I give my pain to God."

I see years of pain in her eyes and want to tell her. "Please, Mom. I

40

don't feel well. I'll make the show later, support those girls."

My brothers are standing by the door with their arms crossed. They know I'm not sick. Myron sticks out his tongue, mouths, "Lucky," and I feign a wave of severe discomfort.

"Fine, Molly May. I don't have the strength to drag you right now. Are you too precious to do a few things for me while we're gone?" Mom asks, over-applying her powdery pink lipstick without a mirror.

***

An hour later, my fingers are oily with the butter that coats the glass pan. I try to move the knob with my elbow, but it keeps slipping, so I use my wrists to turn on the water. I'm washing my hands, when I see Rattle. He says something.

"Didn't hear you," I say, nodding to the water. I pour the crust mixture into the pan and slip it in the oven before sitting next to him at the round table.

"I'm heading out. Your mother won't be happy, but we just spent two hours talking about it, and I didn't budge, so she'll figure it out. Don't let her come after me." His backpack is settled on the table next to him. He's counting out fives and placing them in envelopes. "How long for those lemon bars?"

I shrug. Rattle's eyes are like brown and green marbles. Ribbons of color weave through them, and when he stares, it's like looking at a stuffed animal. "It'll be a while. Rattle, what, um ... what do you think of me becoming a cop?"

I expect him to laugh. Instead, he looks uncomfortable. "Don't let your mom follow me, got it?"

"You'll be long gone by the time she gets home."

"She's probably parked around the corner." He stands, pulling up his belt, which is too loose on the last loop. "Being a cop is like getting paid for the bullshit we live through. Might as well be the one with the gun ... I say go for it, kid."

I nod, seriously, appreciating his pragmatism. Everyone has their moments. I can't help imagining Allie with a gun, a vigilante. I grab a wooden spoon and hold it tight as I begin to mix the lemon juice and sugar. Mom's handwriting is hard to read, so I pull up a recipe online as

41

Rattle hurries out the door. "See you later, Officer," he says.

"10-4," I say, reaching for a paper towel. I'm glad Rattle stuck to his plans. Mom can be a bully, and bullies need to lose sometimes.

The lemon mixture settles on the crust evenly because I pour slowly. I'm careful when I replace the pan and set the timer. While I wait, I jump up on the counter and cross my legs with my laptop perched on my knees. I open the review sheet I was given, but it appears nothing more than a storm of numbers and letters paired with confrontational questions. I stare at them, moving them around, sure that I'll never be an accountant. I open another window and start to type on a blank page, a letter that I don't realize will stop my sister's correspondence altogether for a while.

Hey, Allie. Come get me? Mom won't know.

That was just bad luck, that one time she caught us. Please visit me. Nothing going on here. Mom does good things sometimes, you know. She's crazy, but she has soft moments. Sometimes. Our brothers are still crazy.

I'm thinking of becoming a cop. I'll make pretty good money, and when I took the Career Profile Assessment, it assigned me either that or accountant, and I hear suicide rates are higher among accountants. Plus, I suck at math. Maybe I could help your movement somehow, organize a "police for peace" movement? Did I mention I miss you?

Love, MM.

Simple. Lemon bars are simple, but there is something dynamic about the soft layer of powdered sugar, the tartness of the lemon, and the earthy sweetness of the crust as they melt onto the knife I use to loosen a rectangle, then another. What remains on my knife is all I will be able to eat. If I take an entire piece, Mom will know I'm not sick.

I lick the knife, my tongue jumping at the metallic segue to layered sweetness. I don't hear them. I feel the flavors dancing on my tongue, leaning over the counter with the knife in my mouth, breaking every single kitchen rule Mom has ever instituted—no laptop on eating area, no elbows on counter, no eating from the pan.

Mom yells, and I use it to my advantage. As she screams, I breathe deeply, hearing each word hurled at me as though it is being hurled from behind the wall. My brothers run upstairs, and when the lecture is over, I carefully slice through the perfect rectangle, releasing two lemon bars. I plate them.

"I didn't hear you come in," I say, worrying that I had I blacked out. Maybe I really was sick?

"That's not the point ..."

"Mom, I didn't hear you come in," I say again, seeing the tears before I feel them. They swell in my sightline, sting, and I am grateful for them because when they fall down my cheeks there is clarity. I cup my ears and release. I push hard against them and let go. There is no ocean sound when I cup my ears, barely a whoosh. I only feel my cool fingers, the base of my palms.

***

The doctor's office is cold. "The world doesn't want you to hear it for the time being," Dr. Rash says in a soft voice. Allie would say something comforting. *There are other ways to hear the world.*

As the tests begin and pamphlets are collected, I focus my eyes. Rattle returns and leaves again, and I see why Mom didn't want him to go that first time. One night he spends at home, I catch him flipping between political news, nodding angrily at the TV. Mid-channel change, I ask him if there are deaf police officers. It's a thing I've asked every search engine online, to no clear answer. I even emailed the precinct downtown, to a baffled response: "I'm sure you can do something. We'll investigate it. Is this for a school project?"

Rattle doesn't hesitate to answer. He never does, and I appreciate this. He says it'd be an attribute. "The less you hear, the better. People are full of shit. Criminals are especially full of shit."

***

My letters, folded into tightly packed triangles, collect on the tree out back that week; they collect until Mom rakes them up with the leaves and stuffs them in a thick bag, the few that dislodged during a windstorm. I watch, horrified, then thankful, that she doesn't read them.

I watch the news with Rattle, waiting to see my sister. I look for her in papers, on flyers, and when we ride anywhere at all. We've always had a silent way of communicating, Allie and me, connecting transcendently, ignoring distance and time. *Come get me.*

I take a series of audiologic tests, knowing, as I do in math class,

43

that I flunked the hardest parts. After my acoustic reflex tests, I sit next to a computer screen with electrodes on my head. I feel like a science experiment as I wait. "We're testing for your biological response to sound, Molly May. These are called the Auditory Brainstem Response and Auditory Steady State Response tests. ABR and ASSR for short."

The doctor's voice is clear. He must be screaming. I watch his mustache move with his upper lip. It's thick hair, like darkened straw. He smiles and hands me a magazine with the headline "Could War Be in America's Future?" It's not a question.

I wait for an answer. We all wait. Rattle returns from his third trip to the casino with a modest winning of a couple hundred, and you'd think the guy just won a million. He struts around the house like a champ, until my medical bills arrive in the mail. They only reflect the tests, and Rattle knows better than to show Mom.

"It's time we got you a job, Scout," he says. "I called insurance, and it'll be about five-hundred dollars after all they take care of. Maybe more. Not sure if you know this, but we barely have this two hundred. So. Job? It'll avoid the caterwaul."

I know exactly what he means. "Done deal, but only if you don't call me Scout again," I say. He pats me on the shoulder, and I feel my own eyes becoming marbles, hardened and glassy, as I stare at him.

***

"She may still have a shot at saving her hearing," the doctor apparently told my mother over the phone, but when Mom recounts this, she also says the hearing aids cost "a shit ton, Molly May. You really need to get a job."

"I'm working on it." I've already applied at the grocery down the street and as a receptionist at a small art gallery. I have been searching online for dog-walking gigs, and I'm even desperate enough to try my hand at babysitting. I run through my mental inventory of options. She says it again, and I hear her clearly, but I don't respond. She is puzzled, maybe unsure if I've heard her, and this gives me power. Mom doesn't repeat herself to test me.

I pull up my resume and cover letter on the laptop, trying to ignore my brothers as they argue over who gets to use the iPad. Mom sips iced coffee from a martini glass and glares at me.

Keep looking, Molly May. Put in 20 applications today. Make goals, reach them. Mom writes this in front of me on a piece of notebook paper, then holds it up to my face. She is cradling the martini glass in her other hand and looks ridiculously harsh, and for some reason this makes me smile instead of worry. Maybe I can embrace this silence. Maybe silence *is* power.

I imagine I might have some freedom myself one day. I smile at Myron and Joey, who are peeking out at us from the stair railing. Myron angles his head against the wood, staring out as though from a prison cell, looking confused. Joey gives me a lipless smile, the sort that says *Whaddayagonnado?*

I begin finding notes everywhere but the oak tree, from everyone but Allie. I tease out a lot of things about my life. I read lists and requests, mostly penned by Mom. My family begins to read each other's notes, too. Rattle and Mom's notes have hearts or skulls on them, depending on the day. My hearing impediment has started a new wave of communication in our home. Mom's late nights are now things she boasts about. *I am working toward my goals. Focus, and the results will appear,* she writes mysteriously, leaving sticky notes on the fridge. I believe she's writing them to herself. *These long days are going to pay off.*

Weeks pass, and I hand notes to my instructors to get front-row seats and special allowances. I begin to watch body language closely, making a study of it. I watch military recruiters glide down high school hallways with rigid determination. I watch boys with slumped shoulders look up to them without looking *at* them. I watch police officers stroll around our neighborhood, their guns resembling extra limbs protruding from their hips. I see no women in uniform, let alone a woman with a hearing aid, and I imagine myself filling this gap—no matter how unlikely—walking with intention, not swagger. I take note of everything I want to emulate, everything I want to leave behind.

With my senses dulled, I notice nuance in class. The way certain instructors at school favor certain legs when they stand. Some suck their teeth or cross their arms when frustrated. I can predict fistfights between girls before the first punch is thrown, and I begin tipping kids off so that the crowds can gather more efficiently. I see Mom lean toward Rattle when they speak, even when they argue, and I watch him lean away. She loves him, and he's harder to read. I see their fights coming like clouds collecting in the sky before a storm. More and more, he leans away.

I hear enough to get by while we wait for a more definitive answer. I see specialists who say I don't need devices, I need surgery. I bag groceries and learn some basic signing, just for the hell of it. There is a surgical procedure available that will, if not restore my hearing, keep my inner ear from incurring further damage.

I save money. I help pay the bills. Rattle goes to the casino. I save money. Mom asks for loans so that she can make investments into her mysterious fund, but I never see her spending. I save money by not letting them know when I get a raise. I save money and wait until, eventually, I have a pre-op examination and am cleared for surgery. The mustachioed doctor suggests I get in now, as health-care rates are expected to soar, but he wants to see me one last time before we schedule.

I wonder what my sister would think if she knew I can't hear the world the way other people can. She'd want to be there if she knew a surgeon's scalpel would be so near my brain. I haven't heard from her in weeks, and I'm worried.

I wait, glancing out the window as Joey does his best Charlie Chaplin to cheer me up. He's obsessed with Chaplin now, and his impression of The Tramp is brilliant. I clap, fast and hard so that I can hear it myself. I type my brother a note on the iPad that I carry around everywhere now, mostly for other people to use, thanking him for being here because sometimes it's better to write. He tips his hat and dances off.

My gaze follows him downstairs toward the TV, which Rattle left on. I make my way downstairs, reluctantly, leaving the window open. "Breaking News" and "Special Alert" careen along the top and bottom of the screen. I watch, hearing static. As the news becomes increasingly dire, mere headlines flashing on the screen, the silence becomes addictive.

"They're fighting. You're screwed," Myron yells near my ear, then rushes off to find and harass our little brother.

If we don't leave now, we'll be late. I close my eyes and relish in the silence. I tell it how little I want to hear from the world. I tell it that I want to run away, like my sister, but not *with* her, because fuck her. She abandoned me. I am stuck in time, unable to grow in this house, and she knows it.

I feel a weight on my shoulder. I know it's my sister's hand, saying "Sorry, Molly May. Sorry. I got you," and because I know it's her, I refuse to open my eyes.

I tell Mom's temporary God how much I hate my sister now, how much I hate my mother and all her big mysterious plans. I confess all my sins, until I hear something drop in the room above. Something thrown, no doubt. I look to the clock and notice how late it is, and I decide to stop waiting. I walk out the front door alone, toward the bus stop, and find my way to the doctor's office. There, I pull up the Academy's application form and feel a heat raging in my belly.

SENSORY DETAILS

Columbus, Ohio—2017

I t's my fourteenth day as a bagger, the first day I can't keep my eyes off the rooster-shaped clock above the candy aisle. I'm still in the probationary period at Swifts, so I do what I can to focus, make a game of it. Each new bag can be optimally filled in less time than the last.

Four cardboard boxes containing crackers, pretzels, pasta, and rice fit safely in a single medium bag. The store's plastic is thin, and I need to position the boxes vertically so that the edges don't cut a hole in it before customer #34 gets to her trunk. Tortilla chips and salsa come down the belt next. The rooster's eyes dart back and forth with the seconds; time seems stuck.

"Would you like help out to your car?" I ask. The woman, who wears a gray hoodie and yoga pants that appear stretched to capacity, has a resting bitch face if ever I've seen one; she nods her head no, but I catch a fleeting smile. It's a tough break, but I get a glimpse of teeth, a slight upturn to the corner of her lips.

When I speak, most people soften. Maybe out of pity. I prefer to believe they smile because I sound charming now, that my voice is melodic like my sister's, but I know better. To me, it sounds like my words are mere echoes, as though my voice is stuck inside a cave.

I watch the clock, slip a magazine into a bag with scented toilet paper. A newspaper is next; I wedge it between the two products so that it doesn't crease. The top story today is the president's air raids over Syria and denial of Russian collusion. I do not process either of these things. I never think too much about political news and world affairs. I just take for granted that we won't blow up, or that if we do, it'll happen before I can hear it.

What news stories do remind me of is my sister. Allie's activism is what led her to find her own way, to run toward her own beliefs. I imagine my sister standing tall—chest to chest with a middle-aged man wearing a red hat, asking him, *What's so great now?* The longer she's away, the more typecast and heroic she becomes in my mind. I've had dreams in which she wears a cape and is covered in angry tattoos.

The next customer thanks me, and I say, "You're welcome" in what I imagine must be a shout, because she widens her eyes before walking away. My hearing loss is due to a mass, an acoustic neuroma that formed in my inner ear. When the doctor showed it to me in high definition, it was the size of a pea. I was by myself when I got the news, sitting in a room with walls the color of eggplant and a simple desk, wondering how such a small thing could be so destructive.

The doctor scratched the back of his neck as I explained that due to extenuating circumstances (I really said *extenuating circumstances*), my mother couldn't be there, but she wanted me to receive the news myself. The doctor, in turn, asked me to sign a form and then typed a note that explained my condition and options. He insisted on calling my mother before handing it to me to take to the billing office.

When she answered, he handed me the paper and narrated as I read, then waited for questions. *Why must I wait for the permission of a woman who is too busy to be at her own daughter's appointment? Mom's new God: I wish I had a different mother.* After reading through my diagnosis and recommendations, I said "thank you" in my clearest voice.

"You're welcome, young lady." He spoke to me as one grown-up to another; no exaggerated lip movements, no sympathy, just pure professionalism. "Wait here." He gestured to a seating area. A pile of *Foreign Affairs* magazines sent a chill down my spine. My sister used to devour this magazine, as did my father. My sister and I found his old subscription more than five years ago and laughed at each other as we tried to sound out the words and names of world leaders with consonant and vowel combinations that confused our tongues.

Allie, older and always the autodidact, had been more persistent. She read the magazines late into the night, trying to make sense of the content, then the world. "There are such obvious patterns, Molly May. Political scientists aren't blindly devoted to parties. They look at patterns. I don't understand why we repeat so many bad decisions," she would say.

My sister eventually got her own subscription, along with a few other magazines, and she read each issue online. Had Allie stayed in school, I'm sure she'd be majoring in government by now. She knows more about policy than most college-educated adults.

As I sat in the doctor's office the day of my diagnosis, I thought about what it might be like inside my sister's head; I had once coveted her rage and drive, her desire to change the world. For my part, there was mostly fear from reading about the threat of war with North Korea, or worse, complacency. Allie always found such things enraging, a reason to fight. She treated the news as fuel. Meanwhile, I figured most news was a good reason to never leave my room, or to get an occupation in which I could at least hold a gun to protect myself when the violence came full circle.

Worrying over such topics was an endless battle in my mind then. Now, with the volume of the world lowered, I can think more clearly. I plan to join the police force, a plan I've had for years, though I bet I'll spend more time at the precinct than anywhere outside if I can't stall this hearing loss.

A half hour passed, and Mom didn't arrive to pick me up from my appointment. An hour passed, and she was called again; it had been enough time that I could have taken the bus home. I was almost out the door, ready to do just that, when she torpedoed in.

"Holy God, it's a tumor," she hollered, loud enough that I could hear every intonation. She was still in her uniform, a white button-up with a brown stain on the left boob and a pair of tight black pants. Everyone in the office could hear her every intonation; I'm sure of it. The acoustic neuroma itself likely heard her every intonation. She cried as though I'd just been given a terminal prognosis.

The doctor, who nodded at me in solidarity, met Mom's eyes as she sat near the window and assured her I'd be fine. Mom sobbed, near-yelling, "It won't be fine. These visits here are going to put me into bankruptcy. I have a plan for my family. I want my children to do better." She was trying to get a discount. I'd seen this before. If only she were as good an actor as my brother, Joey, it might have worked.

The doctor returned to me then, with a look of sympathy that I knew had more to do with Mom than the tumor. "It'll continue to grow as long as it remains in her body, but it will grow slowly, so you have some time. It is in no way cancerous, and Reception can discuss financing options." I imagined my own calm when dealing with anxious and emotionally unstable people at the precinct. *Yes, Ma'am, I realize your husband cheated on you, but we are here to discuss the repercussions of your actions. No person should cheat, but no person should throw rocks at another person's BMW either.*

"Will she hear in that ear again?" Mom asked. Her eyelashes were bare and her cheeks black from the tear-smeared mascara. I listened to the doctor repeat his assurance.

"I can hear *you*," I said.

"We may be able to salvage what's left of her hearing in that ear, which still seems pretty good, right?" I nodded, shrugged. It wasn't. My hearing was off-balance; it confused my brain and slowed my response. The doctor looked to Mom. "But the sooner we operate, the better. As I said, these tumors often grow."

I stared at him for a while, then looked to Mom. "Mom, you need to wash your face," I said. I can tell her act won't work. I walked to Reception and asked about the payment plan. Only a hearing aid was covered. Surgery was considered elective, for some reason, so I began calculating in my head, figuring that if I was able to funnel 70% of my paycheck from Swifts into a health-care account, I'd have it paid off in a year.

***

It is my twenty-seventh day at work. My shift is only three hours, and I will have to run to get there on time after the last school bell chimes. I sit in the seat closest to the door, waiting. A check for four hundred and thirty dollars is tucked into my front pocket. I feel for it between note-taking in English class, last period.

Mr. Makioka paces in his brown polyester pants, as a sign language interpreter—there for Graham, who sits in the front row next to me— explains his theory behind Gatsby's obsession with wealth and why this is so pertinent in today's day and age. I don't really need the interpreter since I can hear well with my good ear positioned toward the front of the class, but I am enjoying the dual lesson. Learning sign language will probably help me get accepted into the Academy. Maybe my curse will be a blessing.

Mr. Makioka is a short man with wild hair who loves Shakespeare and tells us that old-school methods work. I still hear his voice, but can barely distinguish his trademark inflections. He teaches English at all grades, says the world's citizens are writing more than ever but making less sense. "We're all about speed, not substance," he says almost every class; an interpreter in a purple sweater signs this message, and I laugh—without realizing it—aloud. Her hands look dry, and I think about offering her the lotion in my bag but worry that it might come across as pushy. Offering a stranger lotion is something Mom would do.

When the bell rings, I run as fast as I can to work, barely making it on time. I am sure I will see Allie. I am sure of this every day, that she will just show up as though she were never gone, but all I see is the rooster-shaped clock, the slowness of time, the over-salted, over-fatted Midwestern groceries of choice. I almost clap when I see Swiss chard and shallots. I smile at everyone and choose to take a vow of silence this day to see how people react. They do not.

***

It is my forty-fourth day of work, and I have surgery scheduled a month out. I made the appointment myself. My mother won't spend a dime, which makes her more supportive. "You have to understand, Molly May. I have big plans for us. I've been saving." I do not watch the clock this day. I'll remember this later, how I didn't watch the clock.

I own a cheap hearing aid that whistles at times, and today I remove it. It is on this, my forty-fourth day of work, that I get the news. Rose, the team lead on shift, pulls me aside and moves her hands through her short bob. A recently retired janitor named Bud had called Mom, said he'd found my sister sitting on a bench, rocking back and forth. She'd been beaten and was bleeding out, so he rushed her to the hospital because he didn't want to call the police. The hospital called the police twenty minutes later, and they called Mom. She called Rose on her way to the hospital and asked that I be let off work early; she didn't ask to speak to me.

"I'm going to break protocol and drive you," Rose says. She takes a deep breath. "Don't tell anyone."

The news is too much to digest; it sounds like fiction, like one of my daydreams gone awry. As we ride, Rose tells me more. "That man who found her had just shopped at our store for oatmeal and a gallon of milk, I guess. Not sure why your Mom told me that, but it sure is coincidental, eh? I guess he's being questioned since he didn't call the police." Rose's voice is pitchy, but I can hear her clearly in the car. I focus on her chapped lips moving, but I don't fully take in this information. Mom would offer her lip gloss. Allie would offer her water.

Rose leans in toward me at a stoplight. I like to see faces up close— the wrinkles that distance hides. I like the moles and indentations, the realness of people. "Go on now," she says, and I realize that we're not at a light at all. We're here. There are hospital lights everywhere.

"Thank you," I say. Maybe I yell. I nudge a few times to get the door open, and when I try to close it, she tells me that I need to really slam it.

***

My family is a cluster of chaos in the waiting room, a bundle of odd shapes. The hospital smells of lemon and bleach. "Funny thing. I don't usually eat breakfast," a man says to my mother. He's wearing house shoes—half-slipper, half-sandal—and baggy jeans with a button-up shirt. Mom doesn't appear to be listening. Her eyes are feral. As though catching my thoughts, she quickly regroups, standing to introduce me to Bud.

"He found your vigilante sister. The fool." She turns to Bud. "Her, not you."

I shake his hand, sit with my good ear facing him and the other one facing Mom. Rattle, my mother, and my two brothers are all in this sterile waiting room, and we all look confused and desperate for the facts. We take up the entire corner, a fourth of the room.

My sister is eighteen and has no insurance, but they can't refuse to treat her, because she was bleeding rather heavily and could've died. Bud says he believes she was stabbed and beaten, maybe more. I have yet to see her, and there are a dozen different possibilities. I imagine the sister I knew who ran away from home, who left notes for me when she could. Only me. I imagine a slightly premature version of my sister with a small wound on her arm. I imagine her fighting off dozens, as though in her own movie. I imagine an older version, too old, looking like Mom, with her forearm sliced to pieces, her arm nearly severed. A dog's teeth tearing at her skin, my shero lifting her fist toward the sky.

"What did the police say?" I ask, somewhat accusatorily.

"Fuck the police. Can't trust them," Bud says. Mom mouths *crazy* from her seat, and I ask Bud another question.

"How bad was it?" I watch his lips. He gives a funny look as he answers. The room is full of dead silence. Even Myron and Joey, my younger brothers, sit unmoving and in apparent shock. Joey's large brown eyes remind me of cow eyes, the poor animals that are kept in the agricultural department of the college near work. They must test antidepressants on these cows, because they look equal parts spacy and content, and at times enraged. All these things commingle in my brother's eyes.

"Who did it?" Rattle asks, but we've already established that Bud doesn't know. It's a question I will ask myself endlessly, but right now I just want to see her.

"I've seen worse, that's for sure. Problem is, whoever it was got her good." He makes a stabbing motion. "Lots of bleeding. She's a little beat up, too. She looked like a drunkard when I ran into her. I didn't even see her there, not till I got near the bench. Scared the living shit out of me, wavering like that. I've been watching too much of that *Walking Dead* show; you know it?"

Rattle stands. "Thanks for bringing her in, man," he says, patting the guy on the back before making his way to the vending machine. He contemplates the selections with his hand on his chin. There's not much to choose from, and I know he'll get the Reese's Peanut Butter Cups, because he always does. Rattle doesn't really know my sister. He started dating Mom just after Allie ran away, but he seems especially intrigued by her now. Maybe because he wants to run away himself at this point. My eyes settle on the snake tattoo that adorns his arm. He presses a few buttons and I watch the orange package fall.

Myron and Joey stare at each other, a contest. Myron blinks, Joey says something, and Myron punches him. They are sitting across from me, numbly trying to be my usually annoying brothers. Mom, who is sitting next to me, is talking to Bud, who says, "Well, I write crime novels, so I have a stomach for blood."

I look down at my Converse, unsure what to think, what to expect. I walk over to a pile of reading materials and see only fashion magazines, gossipy news about celebrities I don't care about. There is a golf game on the television in the corner. I imagine the rooster's eyes darting back and forth at work.

"My sister is home," I say, aloud, not realizing a doctor is approaching. He taps me on the shoulder and makes a sweeping motion, and I realize he must think I'm completely deaf.

"We need to keep her overnight. She lost a lot of blood, but she's healing like a champ."

"Like a champ," Mom repeats. "Good Lord!" I look to Mom, waiting to see if she wants to go in first. She doesn't budge. "One deaf, one dumb. What did I do to deserve this?" she asks. She says it quietly, looking up with rage, and her voice echoes in my skull.

She's your daughter; your daughter is home, I want to say, as loud as possible. Everyone in the room will stare at me, and I'll repeat. Even with the feeling of blood at the surface of my cheeks and my muscles going rigid, I'll repeat. Mom's eyes will narrow, so I will look to my brothers, who will repeat. *She's your daughter. Your daughter is home!* Mom will be jarred from her self-importance and, for once, feel the pang of motherhood.

This doesn't really happen, of course. What really happens is that Mom points her finger at me, says, "Watch it, *little girl*." In the cold, unlikable world, my brothers and I are ushered back to see my sister, and Mom continues to bitch as though she's some sort of martyr and we are the source of her torture.

As I walk into Allie's room, holding my brothers' hands, my own anger parts like a curtain. My tears are violent and unrelenting; my sister, reduced to this battered body on a hospital bed, appears small for the first time in my life.

She looks as though she's asleep, but I know she isn't. Her eyelids, fringed with those thick lashes, flutter. I sit on a chair that is positioned right next to her. Myron tries to wiggle Allie's toe, but Joey slaps his hand away. Joey stares at Myron with just enough threat that my larger, more aggressive brother backs away and sits near the window. Today is a day of reversed roles.

Joey follows. Myron looks down at his shoes. Joey watches me. He's been learning sign language and he says something from across the room, but I don't catch it because my eyes are fixed on a piece of his hair that is sticking straight up and to the right, like a finger pointing. I stand up and go smooth it down, as I know Allie would.

My sister's eyes flutter again. I want to wiggle her toes myself, jar her from the thoughts I imagine she's thinking. Her face shows no injury, but her head is propped up on a circular pillow as though she was hit on the back of her head.

"Allie, I'm glad you're home," I say.

Joey and Myron amble up to my side when I begin to speak. Myron makes a shushing gesture, finger to lips. I must be loud. My sister's eyes flutter a third time; her breath is steady, uninterrupted.

When I turn around at the nurse's call—those ten minutes feel like seconds—Mom rushes into the room. I am rushed out. I can see her speaking to my sister as the nurse asks me to sit with Rattle. I look back to see if Allie is responding and don't notice even the slightest movement, but her face becomes more still. My mother places the back of her thin hand against Allie's forehead as though taking her temperature, a rare and tender moment. Joey grabs my hand and we walk the length of the hall.

When we sit back down, his lips almost touch my good ear as he says, "I wish I didn't hear some days." I nod. "She hasn't even been gone that long and I feel as though I don't really remember her," he adds. I reach for his shoulder, hugging him tight. Neither of us cry anymore; there are no more tears.

**

It's not just my bad hearing those first few days; it's actual silence. Allie barely speaks, and when she does, her words are flat and distant. She had been beaten, left silent. But I know the silence is temporary.

I smooth her silky brown hair as she sleeps. We share a bedroom again, but it's like living with a ghost. She tells me about her efforts to register more voters, and shares pieces about her life outside these walls, but our conversations are stilted—every story seems to stop short of its conclusion. I know a lot from the letters we traded while she was gone. I know she was part of a resistance movement; she worked all kinds of jobs, just like Mom. She wrote all this in letters, which I read back to her some nights, hoping her words will bring a touch more color to her cheeks.

Her resistance movement had almost landed her in jail, one of the letters said, and I ask her to tell me that story in detail.

"A little at a time, Molly May," she says.

"Who did this to you?"

"I told you I'd come back for you." She smiles at me in a way that makes me think she has this all under control, as though it was all planned; a ploy to gain Mom's sympathy and come back home. But whenever I am at work, bagging food or retrieving carts from the parking lot, I can't help but wonder who did this, and how we can make this person pay. Thoughts become slippery this way.

***

It's Saturday, my sixtieth day as a bagger. I look for my nametag as my brothers play video games on an iPad, passing it back and forth like potheads. Allie watches a daytime talk show with Rattle as I get ready for work. "He's not half bad for a felon," she observes after being home a few days.

Mom is out. She's always out since Allie came back. Mom can't stand to see her first-born in pain and, truthfully, neither can I. During a commercial, I ask again. This time, Rattle is in the room. "Who did this to you, Allie?"

Rattle shakes his head, as though disappointed by my timing. Or redundancy. He and Mom have been asking her daily since she's been home as well, but not during TV time. My sister's heavy-lidded eyes open wide as she looks up at me. The stitches on the back of her head are healing, and her arm, still sewn together, will soon be free of stitches. Mom has found a program for victims of crime and is trying to get her medical bills covered, but Allie's silence has made it difficult to file.

"It's not like we're vigilantes. We're not going to go after him. I just want to know. I mean, was it a random attack or personal?"

Rattle joins in. "Was it one of those extremist assholes?"

My sister goes alert. "Extremist how?"

"Extremist however. Extremist means over the top. Super-rich, super-crazy, super-idealistic." I nod along with Rattle's definition.

"I'm going to kill that bastard," Myron says, after running downstairs with the grace of a buffalo.

"Hey!" Rattle yells. I reposition my new hearing aid as it rings.

"Future extremist," Joey whispers to me, pointing to his older brother, then bugging his eyes out. We four kids are rarely all in the same room. One of us wounded, one slight and sarcastic, one destined for jail (I shouldn't say that about my brother, I know). And me.

I'm sure I look as crazy as the rest with my head perpetually tilted toward the earth. We're the kind of family you'd post pics of after a trip to the general store; hardly the well-dressed, refined bunch that Mom has depicted on her dream board.

***

"It was random. A random act of violence," Allie says. She stands and stretches as though we are talking about the weather, then pats Myron on his head and ambles up to our room. I am not deterred. For the first time in my life, I am on a mission. My sister is a stranger in our home, too timid to be the sister I know.

Late in the afternoon, after a five-hour shift and fifty-two customers with an average of four optimally packed grocery bags, I hand Allie a short letter that tells her how glad I am that she's at home with me. I figure conversation could pick back up, that I can cut through the trauma. "Tell me about your marches again. Tell me about the people you hung out with. Tell me about your boyfriend. I remember you mentioning him."

I watch her read my letter. "Molly May, you are becoming something else," she says, smiling wider than I've seen since she's been back. "I need some time. Can you read to me? I love your voice now. It's transcendent."

"What?"

"Read whatever you want. Something enlightening."

"Fine. But I'm going to ask again." I go online and read the news brief. It's all bad news, so I click on *Science News* and read about the promise of other planets. The way she smiles when I speak makes me think that there just might be some music in me after all. Over the next few weeks, my reading to her becomes our routine. She starts requesting things, emailing me articles. She wants me to read things I barely understand; the new healthcare bill the House passed, which we worry could come to fruition, one that makes basic care optional for states whose citizens have pre-existing conditions. I read the entire article, understanding that I would be excluded from getting insurance due to my diagnosis. She asks me to read her old letters and looks completely transported when I do.

By the time Rattle arrives home with a pizza from Take 'n Bake on a Friday night, I've reached for a trivia book that belonged to our father. I read about trees, aquatic animals, the migration patterns of butterflies, and how to make stained glass. We learn about the world like small children, in awe. I catch Rattle listening in, looking at my sister as though she is an abstract piece of art. She might as well be. "Dad used to study everything," she says. She looks to Rattle. "Get enough for us?"

"So long as Myron doesn't get to it first." It's a mean joke on Rattle's part, but we both laugh. "Come on, kids." Rattle turns toward the kitchen and sets out a few paper plates.

"I wish I could remember him," I tell Allie as we head to the kitchen.

"You will. Everything comes back, good and bad." Allie throws a soft toy at my brothers, who are playing video games in the living room. "You all are going to get hand cramps." She tells them to move, firmly, maternally. A glimpse of her old self.

"We don't have stop times," Myron says, not even looking up from his game. Joey stands, bleary-eyed, and staggers off to his room without finishing his level. "Hey! I was going to beat you," Myron whines; then he glances at the pizza.

My hand is cramped from holding the hardcover trivia book open too long. I realize that it's still in my hand, that I've absently wandered into the kitchen without closing it. I tear off a piece of my paper plate for a bookmark and close it gently. I trace the cover, feeling its coolness. "It's like you're back from war," I whisper to Allie as she picks pineapple off her pizza.

"I need to get myself right, Molly May." The scar on her arm is raised like an angry rose. It looks like someone was trying to carve a message. She traces its length.

"You need to talk about what happened. It'll help."

My sister twists her hair up into a bun and wraps a silky orange scarf around it. She stares at me after releasing this information. We communicate like this, just staring, everyone else oblivious, until I nod.

"Give me some space about it, okay?" Allie says.

"I got pizza," Rattle says, pretending not to hear. "Where is your mother?" he asks me.

Allie sighs audibly. After rolling her pizza slice up and taking a few bites, my sister pushes herself up and walks off, toward our bedroom.

Rattle takes her seat, nearer me. He smells of beer, but not the sour smell of having had too much. He's looking at me as though I'm a piece of art now, a thing to study. It's not a threatening look. It's one that portrays worry and something else, maybe confusion. I stare back, equally confused. "What gives? You're freaking me out."

Tapping his teeth with his nail a few times, he says, "It's time for me to head out."

"Where?"

He shrugs. "Wherever. I need to stay gone this time." He and Mom no longer fight, mostly because she's never home. She leaves him to deal with us, our baggage, and I can tell he doesn't think he can.

"Please don't," I find myself saying, before I can think about what I really mean. How can he leave me? Rattle has been stability for me; he's been the guy on the couch whom we sometimes bail out of jail. In our household, he's the voice of reason.

He scratches his chin and, without a hint of a smile, says, "I wish I could stick around, MM."

I ask him to repeat, and he does. I ask him to verify that he said what I thought he said. He does. I stare at the stubble on his chin, vaguely remembering that my father, too, often had stubble on his chin.

"I don't think I have the patience to deal with your mother, or to be the caretaker of four kids."

"Hey! Allie's grown, and I take care of myself."

"Okay, so you girls take care of yourselves, but these guys." He points at my brothers, who smile at the attention but don't hear because they're in a heated discussion about their scores.

"You're going to leave us here to deal with Mom?" I ask.

"This is *your* bloodline, kid. Besides, you're old enough to head out on your own soon. You have your sister now."

"What about the boys?"

"I don't think I'm a role model, Molly May. And she can't love me, not like I need her."

I stare, waiting for him to reveal more. "Fine. Whatever. Will you — will you still take me to my surgery?" It feels wrong to ask, and I don't push the issue.

***

It's my hundredth day as a bagger, and I am on track to be promoted to cashier. I'm finally sixteen, and I've figured out that the extra dollar and twenty cents each hour, saved, will add up to about forty a week, which is enough to pay off my surgery a month early, so I sign up for the plan. This satisfies Mom because I can still contribute to the household and she can keep her finances in check. Since Allie's attack, Mom's been working more than ever.

My surgery is scheduled during the time I'd usually have lunch break, and I call home to make sure I still have a ride. Rattle says he's on his way and that my sister insists on coming.

"She feels up to it?"

"Yeah. She seems good. Just got out of an appointment with some quack. Look, I'm leaving town tomorrow. Just stuck around for you," he says.

"I appreciate it," I say. *I'd rather Mom leave.*

Rose "overhears" that my surgery is today, and when I hang up the breakroom phone after verifying my appointment, she says, "I'm so happy for you, honey."

"It won't change much, but it will mitigate further damage." I repeat the doctor's words, and my formality makes Rose smile warmly. Rose motions up, a sign that I didn't hear the call for backup assistance. She holds up four fingers.

***

I don't watch the rooster-shaped clock as I bag the groceries on register four. I don't look because I know it's moving too rapidly to be accurate. After hanging my lanyard in the breakroom, a few minutes before Rattle will arrive, I feel my phone buzz and look down to find a text from Mom: *I'm praying for you. Be there after work with the boys.* It's

61

unexpected, and makes me smile, but I know there's a good chance she won't show. I imagine that hospital waiting room, my family loud and the staff trying not to listen.

I clock out by entering my ID in the computer by the coats. When I get up and turn around, my coworkers are staring at me, beaming. They hold what looks like a solid cake but is really two dozen cupcakes topped with thick icing. The bakery manager, Pete, has one end and Rose has the other end.

Rose looks unsteady with the oversized cake, her smile tight, so I quickly clear space on the breakroom table. The cake is pink, strawberry-raspberry, with a beige icing ear in the middle that's detailed with black gelled sugar and surrounded by a few silly plastic decals: a brown dog barking, an old-school radio blaring, and a person with a shower cap on and her mouth open wide, as though she is hitting a high note.

I haven't laughed, really laughed, in a long time, but this cake is ridiculous. It cuts into my nerves. When I take a bite of the tip of my ear in cupcake form, the sweetness is too much. Rose hugs me just as my sister appears in the doorway.

"Come on, Molly May," Allie says as I grab a few cupcakes for my brothers. "Let's fix ourselves up so we can save the world."

FREIGHT

Columbus, Ohio – 2018

I watch with interest as Allie applies for a management position at Swifts. "Managed a team of twenty-six to successful completion of a community-focused project" translates to "Organized and led a protest at the Ohio Statehouse" and "Proficient in business accounting software" means she once did Mom's taxes online. Allie glances toward the hall, then swivels her chair, staring as though waiting for me to notice something. I do not.

"Can you get the door, Molly May?"

I nod, cupping the gauze around my right ear. My brothers never knock, and people don't arrive at our house unannounced. Not long ago, Mom banned all kids and most adults from the property. To this day, she won't so much as allow Girl Scouts on our porch without her consent. She reinforces her rule with a sign on the lawn that says KEEP OUT and, for the hard-headed, a red flag planted in a pot (in place of flowers) near the door.

***

This war with the neighborhood began when Josh and his father moved to the sloping ranch house at the end of our street. At fourteen, less than a year older than Myron, Josh was nearest my brother's age, and they became fast friends. He would show up early mornings, hands in his pockets, grinning with wild eyes as he asked for Myron. If my brother was home, he would run into our house like a feral cat, stumbling up the carpeted stairs. Mom would give him a malevolent look but let him in. That is, until she got the first call at work.

I met my brother on the neighbors' porch that day. Mom was stone-faced and asked me to escort Myron home because she didn't want to look at him. "Bad energy," she hissed. My brother, a touch too plump for his pants, tried to wedge his fingers into the front pocket of his jeans and look angry. His chubby face was rather angelic, which made it comical when he twisted his lips into an angry pout.

"Josh didn't make me do anything. I did it on my own," Myron argued as he pushed himself up from the neighbors' porch.

Mr. Henry, our neighbor, eased back and forth in a rocking chair, only looking up from his iPad to say, "I caught them in the act. The slippery one ran away. I'm pretty sure he's the leader."

"He is not," Myron mumbled, almost tripping on the last step. "I'm not a follower."

"You'd better not be so spineless as to let that kid tell you what to do," Mom answered, staring at Mr. Henry's black Honda, which the boys had decorated with silver stripes. "Sorry for your trouble, Mr. Henry. I'll take care of this. Let me know how much it costs, and I'll write you a check. The boy will pay me back." She pulls Myron closer. "You better believe you'll pay me back."

When we got home, Mom made Myron mow the lawn and vacuum the house. When he was done with that, he had to write her a letter recounting the event and promising he'd never be so stupid again. "Don't forget to sign it." I'd written similar letters, but for less interesting things, such as forgetting the laundry in the washer long enough for the clothes to acquire a musty smell or leaving spots on the dishes. Mom stockpiled all our letters in a large plastic container. Allie had been the only one of us brave enough to refuse to write apologies.

It was on this day, the first day my brother was caught, that Mom created her sign—well, the first iteration—with cardboard and black marker.

"No visitors at all? Not even my friends?" I asked.

"We'll see," she said, setting the sign behind our green couch by the front door. "I'll put this out if I have to. Do you have any friends, hon?" I pretended I didn't hear her, cupping my good ear.

Josh continued to show up after that, only to get the door slammed in his face. In the kid's defense, he tried to make amends, but that just proved how little he knew our mother. When he showed up with cookies on Thanksgiving, Mom lifted her index finger, and as soon as the kid's eyes were locked in, she slowly pointed to his house.

"But my dad's not here, and I just want to come in for a little while—"

I kept an eye on Josh after that. He'd call, asking for Myron to meet him at the mailbox, and I'd glance down the street at them; my brother trying for cool in his droopy sweatpants or shorts, looking like he was headed for the edge of a cliff. I knew my brother was easy to sway. He wasn't stalwart or determined like Joey. He wasn't as talented or smart either, to tell the truth. Bad to say, but truth is truth.

By the time she got the second complaint, again at work, Mom banned Josh from our house for life and asked me to put out the sign she'd created. Then, thinking better of it, she sent out a mass email banning the whole neighborhood from coming to our house when she wasn't around: *I just can't take any chances. I hope everyone understands.*

"Don't you think that's a bit much?" I asked her, after she had me check the email for grammatical errors.

"I'll press charges if I see that little fucker around here, Molly May. That kid's got the devil in him. Just like your father."

"Mom, please stop talking like that," I said, reaching my hand out for a wad of cash. Mom always brought her cash tips home in her bra and handed them to me to count. I always felt a little taller when I was counting that money, but I'd once read an article on the filth of money, how it passes through so many hands and contains myriad germs, including fecal matter.

"Evil has many faces," she said.

Allie wasn't living with us at the time, so I bit my tongue and counted as fast as I could. Mom was always bad-mouthing my father. I remember thinking about how nice it would've been not to hear a thing she said. Funny thing, irony. I can only hear out of one ear now, an ear that's never pointed Mom's way if I can help it.

"One-hundred and thirty-six dollars," I said, folding the bills neatly before handing them back to her and rushing to grab the hand sanitizer.

"On a Friday? Hmm. A hundred and fifty next week. Mark my words. God is good."

***

I finally hear the knocking when I get downstairs. Maybe it's Mom's

Jen Knox

ex coming back to reconcile. Maybe it's Josh, who I still see sneaking around with my brother, and I can tell him to get the hell off Mom's porch. I'm at the door, about to turn the knob, when the knock picks up speed. It's aggressive now. It's an adult knock, or that of a tall, angry kid. Josh is short, much like my brother. This knock rattles the door, and I pull my hand back and lift myself up on my toes so that I can see out the peephole. Two officers with straight faces and straight backs, one young and one old, look at each other as though deliberating. When the door opens, the younger one asks, "Joshua Granges here?" before so much as a hello. I bet he's fresh out of training, and a part of me wants to test him.

"No," I tell him in my loudest voice, then turn my bad ear their way. The right side of my face feels hot where the cloth tape meets my skin, so the coolness outside is welcome. I wait for his reaction.

The older officer, who wears a short gray beard and glasses, moves up a step and looks beyond me. "Hello, young lady," he says, and I shrug. He waits, and I can see the theories forming in his head.

"Tumor," I say quickly, knowing that'll stop any possible questions.

"I'm very sorry to hear. I truly am." He pauses. "Are your parents around?"

"My mother? No."

"Sister?" the young one says, looking beyond me. Something in me tells me to lie.

"No," I say, realizing I'm lying to an officer of the law for no good reason. I want to change the subject, tell them both that I am considering joining the force, and I'd like to pick their brains about the process, but the timing doesn't seem right. "What'd Josh do?"

"Petty kid stuff," the young one says. "Honestly, just stopping by at the end of a shift. We've been asked to scare the kids."

His counterpart glares a moment, and says, "We need to speak to your mother. I don't have a work number for her."

"Yes, sir!" I say, taking his card.

"I'm sorry about your affliction." He points to my face.

"It was benign. Just turns the volume down on the world and makes me talk funny."

"I didn't notice," the younger one says kindly, and I smile flirtatiously.

66

Then he looks past me and leans in. His eyes change. "Let Allie know Griffin says hello."

I feel my face scrunch. Grandma Dee says I'm too transparent, thanks to my overly expressive face, and I can imagine whatever confusion I'm feeling is being conveyed thoroughly. The two officers couldn't care less. They make their way to the Dodge they're driving, and I catch the older one chuckling to himself about Mom's handwritten sign.

"Hey," I call after them. "Can you be a cop if you're deaf in one ear?"

"Maybe. Probably not," Griffin says, then turns to his partner and chuckles. There's no siren or decal denoting police on their car, and still, they leave with purpose, as though a siren is perpetually on and roaring.

"Thanks a lot."

***

My sister must be blaring Bowie, because it seems loud, even to me. I turn the speaker down. "Who's Griffin?" I ask.

She swivels her chair and examines me, as expressionless as I am expressive. Her hair is short and thick now, parted on the side so that it falls like a single wave. "I applied for one of two assistant manager positions. Since there are two assistant manager positions available at the same time, I'm pretty sure that place is messed up enough to need someone quick."

"It is. Who's Griffin?"

"I wonder if they'll let us work the same shift. I don't think I can be your direct supervisor, not legally. Then again, nepotism doesn't really matter in this country, does it?" She turns and opens another window, turning on CNN.

"Allie, I'll keep asking all day."

"I lived with him."

"A cop? Why didn't you just say that?"

My sister stands and narrows her eyes. I see fire. My sister was born during an eclipse, which caused Mom a few-year obsession with astrology that would occasionally return; she did our charts when we were babies and left elaborate notes about the paths our lives would take, jotting her amateur calculations in our baby books. This was all before she found the church. By the time my brothers were born, she was born-again, and I'm

67

pretty sure that in another few years she'll be part of a cult.

I'd examined Allie's charts plenty while she was gone, looking for answers wherever I could. My sister is a fire sign through and through, a Leo with Aries rising. Fire on top of fire.

"How long did you guys date? Was he part of the resistance?"

"Molly May, you're relentless." She smiles suddenly, cutting the tension, then rushes over and begins tickling me like I'm a child.

"I'm basically an adult," I say through gasps. I'm the most ticklish person in the world, and she has me laughing like an idiot. I squirm away, and she stands, examining her application. She nods with the seriousness of a CEO perusing his company's financial prospects, then clicks *Send*.

"So. What'd they want? Myron? He probably filled someone's shoes full of sand."

"They wouldn't tell me."

***

I am Googling "Griffin, officer in Columbus," when Mom is suddenly behind me. I smell her before I hear or see her. Her new scent is one that comes in a bust-shaped bottle and is usually on display at the drugstore, a lavender and vanilla blend, which she over-applies so that it lingers in the house long after she's gone to work. The perfume busts now line up in the bathroom like soldiers. The smell itself, for what it's worth, is lovely. And, right now, terrifying.

"What in the living hell, Molly May? Is your brother in trouble again?"

It comes out before I intend to say anything. "The police were by today, but it was … strange."

"Yeah, they stopped by the restaurant too. Your brother in his room? You make dinner?" She sounds a little too nonchalant about all this.

"Playing video games, I think. We have spaghetti. I can get dinner on in an hour."

"I'm no-carb now. Figure something else out. Here." She hands me a wad of sticky cash. The texture makes me gag. As I begin to count, she collapses in front of the computer, nudging me out of the chair, searching social media sites. "By the way, your brother's going to military school, if there is such a thing around here. I just need to figure out how to enroll

68

his ass."

"What'd Myron do?" I ask.

"What, you don't say hi anymore?" Mom says to Allie, who is gazing out the window.

"Hey, Mom," Allie says, making a sign for me to follow her to our room. She mouths "emergency," and I nod, counting quickly.

Allie tugs on my shoulder, whispering, "I just saw Josh climb out of our bedroom window."

I know whatever we find in there will be horrible. I'm tempted to pretend I don't hear her. But Allie knows better. We storm the room and find Myron, deer-like, looking for an exit but unable to move. I block the doorway. Allie looks under the bed and behind the books on my shelf. A sour smell permeates the room.

"You hid something in here," she says to Myron, flicking him in the center of his head.

"We got to Level 6. It takes weeks to get up a level. I was scared to break into someone else's house and do it. Josh said we should do it here and it'd still count." He crosses his pudgy arms and shrugs.

"Sit down, kid. If you want us to save you from Mom, you'd better explain."

"Sorry. It started simple, but it's getting harder," he says, shifting his feet.

"Explain, kid. What is this game?"

He explains that challenges for Level 1 are easy, things like knocking over trash cans or trying to get a free meal by stuffing a few hairs in your omelet at Denny's. By Level 6, arrests become possible, but "not for anything really bad." Josh apparently reached Level 8, and Myron was determined to catch up.

"So, what did you do in here?" Allie asks through gritted teeth.

"Frog," he says, pointing.

I lift my pillow, and a pale frog belly faces me. What looks like a large toothpick sticks out from its chest. In this moment, I feel something odd: sympathy for Mom. I decide to never have children.

***

Joey, whom we call "the magician" lately because he seems to magically never be around when there's trouble, is staring in the hallway mirror the next morning when Allie positions herself next to him, blocking the bathroom doorway. "Joey, we need you to do some recon," she says. I stand behind her.

"Got to pee, ladies. Move it or lose it."

We step aside and wait at the bathroom door until he comes out, looking far more interested. "All right now, fan club, let's talk business. How much does this gig pay?"

"It pays in karma," Allie says.

"Sorry, but I don't get out of bed for less than fifty dollars," my brother says theatrically.

"I'll pay you cash, then, twenty bucks, and it's a simple job."

"I'm listening. Better be easy for twenty dollars."

Allie pulls on the back of Joey's collar to straighten him up. "We just need you to let us know when you see Josh and Myron together. As soon as you do, text us. We'll give you a code."

"Yeah, and let us know if you hear them talking about the game."

"I'll be your snitch, ladies, but it'll cost you twenty-five, and my code better be cool."

"Text LUCKY, all caps," I say.

***

We research the game, but Myron claims it doesn't have a name. We Google and find nothing, until typing "Level 8, impaled frog." A game called *Tempt Fate* outlines challenges that match up to everything that Myron has done. I even see that "drink every liquid in the fridge" is there, which solves the mystery of being out of both cola and orange juice a week ago. Mom had called me at work with a grocery list containing almost all liquids. When we see the game featured in a cautionary article, with the final challenge warning, we know we must put a stop to it.

There are only four more levels, and we aren't sure whether Myron was telling the truth about his progress. He could be up to Level 7 or 8 by now himself, and that means we need to do something quickly. "What about your friend Griffin?" I ask Allie.

"No. Not him. No police. They're never helpful. They always make things worse."

"Griffin hurt you?" I ask too quickly, too presumptuously, feeling the regret jab me in the side as I say it. My sister doesn't talk about the time she was away. She doesn't look over at me. I watch her tie a colorful scarf around her dark hair, pulling it back effortlessly and without a mirror. She applies brick-colored lipstick and walks out. He did, then. I know.

I follow her. "Allie, we need to trail them. Figure it out. We may not have the luxury of a good sit-down with the kid, and you know Mom will freak out."

"She'll have Myron sent away for some shit like this. It'd be better if he were in a gang."

***

Myron isn't the stealthiest of kids, and this works in our favor. We watch him head to the mailbox at the corner and watch as he waits, staring down at his shoes. We watch Josh run up to Myron like he's going to tackle him, then stop short with a jump, surprising my brother. Myron punches him sloppily, and Josh laughs. They look too goofy to be getting into real trouble. We follow them toward the abandoned elementary school.

"Well, it's either the second story or the landmark. It depends on the level," my sister says, checking her phone. "I mean, there's no way they're up to Level 10. I don't see any backpacks, bags, or evidence of weaponry." We couldn't see the full challenge. You had to sign up for an avatar to see everything, but we could see the location. A map with nameless destinations, such as "second-story building" or "bus stop" appeared when the levels were achieved. Hundreds, maybe thousands have been playing this game, and those who are currently playing—no more than a dozen—showed up in green when they "checked in."

"We should call the police," I say. "I mean, who knows the instructions." A fierce wind hits as I speak, and I can't hear myself at all, not even from my good ear.

"No. We've got this," Allie says, and she lunges toward Myron and Josh. I grab her.

"We need to be subtle," I tell my sister, and she stares at me, squinting her eyes slightly, looking a little too much like Mom. "I mean, we need to be smart. They'll just do it another day if we stop them now. We need to confront them in the act, when they're scared. We need to talk to them, but

71

we have to make sure we know what they're doing."

Just as my sister smiles reassuringly, we hear footsteps, and I turn to find a small man in a hoodie standing behind us. He has a five o'clock shadow and a narrow chin like a child's. *It is a child's chin.* Allie slaps the little man lightly on his arm, and Joey looks up. He's wearing Mom's sunglasses. His disguise is divine. The stubble looks perfectly real, and his hooded, all-black ensemble is the perfect touch. A theater kid to the core.

"This is my sleuth wear. Thought you two wanted me on the case."

"We did. But only at school, goofball. You should go home," I say.

"Great greasepaint, though," Allie says. "Ten out of ten."

"My stylist helped me." My brother bows with a flourish and turns on his heel as he continues. "Fine by me. I should rehearse anyhow. I'm Hook—the Captain to you." He winks, and I rush after him with arms open. As he sprints, I feel my sister's nails dig into my forearm.

"They're gone! We blinked, and those little fuckers disappeared."

We jog toward the school, keeping an eye out for them. I whisper to Allie to listen for the both of us, but I do hear things. I hear the swoosh of cars on High Street and the faint sound of church bells and a train. By the time we get to the playground, we see the little hoodlums running down Summit, toward a floodplain. My sister has her cell poised and pointed ahead like it's a magnet of some sort.

"We have to hurry. If they get past the green, they can hide in the trees."

"We should call the police," I say again.

I haven't run this fast in a long time and my calves are tightening. I realize that Myron and Josh are headed to the train tracks, and my chest rattles as I take jagged breaths. Both of us pick up our speed. We're far enough away that they can't hear us, but Allie is calling out Myron's name.

I hear it louder now, the rhythmic and outdated chugging of the freight train. I read once that most of the trains in this area are transporting either feed for livestock or oil, and I imagine the twenty thousand tons of steel reverberating against the rails. The final level instructs players of the game to tempt fate, and it all becomes clear how real this is. Tempting fate means believing in it, or not believing in it at all. Testing fate would be more accurate.

My sister is several paces ahead of me, her longer legs carrying her forward, the scarf around her head loosening and waving behind her like a tail as she runs. It is suddenly free, catching the wind, and I am watching it waver as I stumble. Landing hard on my hip, I twist to get back up and realize that not only can I hear the train, but I can see it. I watch as Myron and Josh both balance on the rails, arms up like superheroes. Josh is a few feet in front, gesturing toward the train to come on. In this moment, I remember him on our porch with cookies.

Once I'm on my feet, I can see I won't make it to the tracks in time, and my sister is going to be close. Time and space expand and contract as I watch my sister throw herself toward Myron, and their two bodies roll off the track just as the train rushes through. The graffitied cars go on forever. I drop to the ground to see under the cars and make out movement on the other side.

I call Mom at work and don't even hear her responses as I report that she needs to come home and send police to the train tracks on the other side of Hudson Elementary. I tell her we caught Myron doing something horrible, and he may be injured. The train moans as it flies by, never-ending, flattening everything in its path. And when the caboose finally arrives, a new reality arrives.

I finally see my brother and Allie huddled together by the train tracks, my sister's arms sheltering our brother from the brutal scene. I feel only gratitude. I can barely see what remains of Josh, nothing more than parts of a machine. His cellphone was destroyed, but part of it had been driven into his hand by the force. The slight kid with pale hair and a menacing smile, the one Mom banned from the house, was mowed down by the train, and no more than seconds before he was, he'd posted a picture of it to the gaming site. Someone had won, and over a thousand anonymous comments came in, most of which offered praise for Josh. The train was so close, and in the fleeting moment he took the photo, he knew he'd won.

We thought they had been on a lower level. We thought there was no way that they would really try.

That night, the news flashes pictures of Josh with his grandmother. He'd quickly become the poster child for dangerous online games that told kids they were just part of a pattern, a pattern that couldn't be disrupted no matter what. Myron is arrested and must appear in juvenile court a few weeks after the incident. Mom can bail him out but refuses. "Why would I bail him out? I'm the one who put him in the program. He needs to be scared straight."

When he is ushered away, his head hangs like a bag of sand. My brother is sentenced to six months in juvenile detention as part of a "From Criminal to Community Leader" program. Mom stares at him with dead eyes as he leaves.

***

We attend Josh's funeral as a family. There is a candlelight vigil. I hold Joey's hand, which trembles. We stay close to each other, closer than we've ever been, and from a distance we watch Josh's father crumble.

"I called that kid evil," Mom says at last, as she examines the boy's image. "I called that kid evil, but he was just a kid."

For the first time since she's been home, Allie embraces my mother the way she used to. She tries to shelter her the way she tried with Myron, and something in our family dynamic shifts.

***

The day my bandages are cut, I am told that there will be only a slight improvement in my hearing as a result of the removal of the tumor that has been blocking the external auditory canal, and I am fine with the news. I am not yet ready to hear the world, I tell the doctor, or I think it, as he goes over my prognosis. My sister is with me, fiddling with one of Myron's fidget spinners. Mom is supposed to pick us up, but she's late. We watch the television in a waiting room that is becoming all too familiar, and Myron appears on the screen.

This is the first time I've ever seen a family member on the news. He's part of a special that is designed to warn parents about dangerous online games. He has been interviewed on national news and made into a reluctant celebrity from his hold in juvenile detention, but I see his spirit dimmed. Something is missing in his eyes; a light. He explains that it is just a game, and when you think about it, just a philosophy lesson. He says this, but these are not my brother's words. My brother appears thoughtful and tragically brilliant in the interview, but all I can see is the kid behind the words, the kid who rushed down toward the mailbox with

74

baggy sweatpants. All I can see is his desire to find a place in the world.

***

As I enter the blocky, windowless building, I imagine I am at the airport, heading to a warm island where I am served overly sweet alcoholic drinks in overly large plastic cups without being questioned about my age. I can almost see the indigo water and sky filled with yellow and orange brushstroke clouds as I recall my father's one story about visiting a beach in Florida, where he almost stepped on a jellyfish and learned to swim in the same day. When one dies young, a life must be efficient, I suppose.

My experiences come slowly and are spread out, which makes me think I'll live forever. Walking through a metal detector as a man turns my cell over in his hands reminds me of the one time I was at the airport, watching Grandma Dee and my father board a plane to visit a cousin I never met. I crave water and travel. We've been to Lake Erie, and though both the Olentangy and Scioto river waters run through my hometown, converging near Mom's house, my only view of ocean water comes from online videos and screensavers.

These images rotate in my mind as we sit on small plastic chairs that remind me of middle school. Allie and I have come alone. Mom refuses to visit, but she has sent a letter that I am not to open but am supposed to hand to Myron as soon as I see him so that I do not forget. My brother is serving nine months in this facility. He is now going to school online, and his credits will transfer back to the high school near our house.

I have been reading a lot of articles on how to act around those who are in pain. When I see Myron, I will listen with my entire body. I will nod reassuringly. I will smile warmly. LNS. Listen, nod, and smile. I will tell him that I love him unconditionally and that he will have a life after this. If he cries, I will support him. I am not sure whether we can hug. A security guard is telling us the rules now, but I can't hear him.

"Are we allowed to hug?" I ask.

"I just covered that," he mouths, handing me a pamphlet with pictures. One image is of two stick figures shaking hands next to a thumbs-up. The next is of two stick figures hugging next to a thumbs-up. The final picture is of one stick figure placing a bag of something in another's pocket. This one has a thumbs-down next to a picture of two stick figures behind bars.

We wait. Allie yawns; the tendons in her neck tighten. A slow whirring seems to rise from the floor. I look around and see two young boys around Myron's age staring at each other with an odd intensity. I can't tell if they are flirting with or warning each other. One of the boys is in a blue smock that looks like the sort of thing a surgeon would wear. The other is in street clothes, jeans and a jacket. I look around for coffee, knowing the chances are slim.

My sister holds the number we were given: 46. An announcement requests 30, and I sigh audibly. I don't realize how loud I am; my hearing loss is more noticeable indoors. Everyone, including the two boys, stares at me. I've learned to smile when this happens. It happens often, and it used to make me look down at the floor, my shoulders caving. Now I just smile at those who stare. I am less hearing-abled, but I own it.

"Own your journey," Allie always says. Even though I'm not so sure she's able to do the same, I know that when she tells me something, I had better listen.

Allie jots #MeToo on a notebook that she carries everywhere. I'm surprised the small pen that fits inside the cover isn't taken from her. She writes the letters big and fills in the space around them, adding crosshatch shadows.

"I didn't do anything," my brother says as soon as we walk into what looks like a classroom. I see him for the first time without the trademark red in his cheeks. He looks sort of gray, actually, as though he's missing vital nutrients.

"Everyone in here is innocent," I say, smiling. Allie offers us a slow clap, and even the guard chuckles a bit.

"You all have twenty minutes," the guard adds.

"No, really. I was trying to push Josh out of the way," my brother insists. He says it in a near whisper; no showy plea for attention and pity. He says it genuinely.

I slide the letter over to him and see a wave of relief pass over his face as he reads. Mom must have sent some reassurance, something kind or, though I can't imagine it, empathetic.

"She's getting me out of the program," he says.

When Mom picks us up, she says nothing, doesn't ask how it went.

She says almost nothing for the duration of the ride, hiding behind large sunglasses. When we arrive home, I see the makeshift sign in the trash on the side of the house.

COFFEE

Columbus, Ohio – 2019

"I have a plan," Allie says. She positions two slices of white bread on a paper towel. After smearing them with butter and adding a healthy sprinkle of cinnamon-sugar, she microwaves the slices until they become the texture of wood.

"What kind of plan?" I ask. The room fills with the warm aroma as we lower the sound of a news story about the government shutdown.

"You want out of here?" She hands me a slice of hot bread, immediately wiping away the crumbs that fall on my knee. I take a cautious bite. It's like eating an over-sugared, over-large piece of crust.

"I have a year of school."

Allie breaks off a corner of her hot bread and examines it before placing it on her tongue. Her eyes are fixed, patient and intense. "All the more reason to leave now. Look at us, M. We're eating sugary bread for lunch. This is the beginning of the end."

"I'll pick up some fruit today. I have a short shift."

"That's not the point. Fruit is not the point."

I open my mouth wide, hoping to pop my ear. It always feels like it needs to pop. Unhinging my jaw a few times before giving up, I say, "I know. But Mom might—"

The room turns from comfort to cold, department-store cold, as soon as I mention her. I smell the sharp notes of her perfume intermingle with the cinnamon-sugar before I hear her. I cover my hearing ear.

"Mom might what?" she says, and I don't move. She stands behind me, and I can feel her there, the warmth. My blood swells.

–freak out.

"Molly May was just saying that you're working tomorrow, can't pick us up from Swifts, and it's supposed to rain," Allie says. When Mom turns toward the coffee pot, my sister winks at me. I shrug, tracing the roof of my mouth with my tongue where tiny scratches remain from the tough bread. I get hot chills when I'm uncomfortable, and right now I am shaking from the contradictions in my body.

One of the walls in the kitchen is exposed brick, which lets cool air seep in. I scoot my chair away from the wall and try to ignore the ringing in my right ear, which is incessant.

"Climate change is a bitch," Allie says, taking off her sweater.

"Thought it was supposed to make things warm." Mom turns on her heel. When Allie doesn't take the bait, Mom looks at both of us with eager eyes. "Listen. You two are going to help me. We need to own something," she says, purposefully raising her voice a decibel above Allie's. Mom's hair is in a high bun that cascades down on the sides. She picks at her nails, which are short and tasteful this week. Sometimes they're long and sharp, like weapons. Lately, they've been square and soft, with simple French manicures or pale polishes. I noticed the shift ever since she began to work long catering events at work, events that sometimes take all night to clean up, she says.

She has a plan, I can tell.

Mom reaches for my forearm and scratches it lightly. The tips of her nails are like tiny ceramic plates gliding across my skin, and I fight the urge to pull away. I say, "I thought you hated this house."

"This place is a horror show; that is correct, Molly May. We should own land. A business. In fact, you girls should stop wasting your time and energy catering to Swifts. Some other family owns that. We could start our own. A bakery maybe or a salon. I'm almost *there*, girls. I'm almost to my goal. My savings. It's time to start the legacy project."

"That's what your savings is for?" I ask.

"That's part of it," Mom says.

"No way would I run a salon," Allie says, leaning back confidently, elbows on the counter. I'd have been yelled at for putting my elbows on a cooking area, but no more words are exchanged. Mom glares. Allie doesn't budge.

"What's the other part?" I ask.

Mom smiles slyly. "It's the American Dream, and it's right there for the taking. You know, people come to this country and make it—get the house, the fence, the car and pension—in a single generation. Meanwhile, you girls have no initiative because you've been given everything."

"Given everything?" Allie interrupts. "We've been given everything, Molly May. Who knew?"

"So, Alison. MOLLY MAY ... children of privilege ..." Mom cracks her neck and rolls her shoulders back a few times, as though she's in the boxing ring. "We need to strategize. Let's put our heads together and focus. I want you both to read *The Power of Personal Leadership*—a great book! I just finished it, and it lays out the whole truth of our existence. It says that if you do not act on the ideas you have, you might as well not have them at all." When we don't indulge this potential conversation, Mom goes into full-on pitch mode.

"Think about it, girls. It's like *that guy* we all know who says he thought of the smartphone before smartphones were invented, and he's shitty about it into old age, like he's been robbed of the idea. Ideas mean nothing if they don't take form. A guy can't say he invented the cell unless he actually went to the trouble of patenting and hiring some designers and investing ... you get the idea."

"What if he doesn't have the money to do all that?" Allie says.

Myron still lives in a state-funded program for boys, which means he must attend meetings and share a room. He has about six months left "inside," and the first thing he told me when we last visited was that he couldn't understand how people lived before technology. "Boredom is torture. Being alone all the time or caged up with crazies," he said. Technology is why he's locked up, of course, but I didn't bring that up. I didn't bring up the fact that the facilities looked more like a summer camp than a prison either.

"If we must start a business, let's start a café. We can call it Red v. Blue," Allie says.

Clapping her hands, Mom says, "How patriotic! Red and Blue. I love it. Where's your brother?"

"Red v. Blue is what I said. Joey's at band practice, Mom. I was being facetious."

"Well, he can be the coffee maker. Why *not* a political café? Politics sells. It can be a place for people to come together."

"The barista," Allie corrects.

"I can see it," I say, smiling at the unrealistic image in my mind of my brother frothing milk as Mom and Allie make scones and ring up the first in a long line of customers. "One side of the café can be all in blue, the other in red."

Allie nods along, over-enthusiastically, as she looks to Mom. "Why not? We can have a stage on the blue side for poetry, and you can have—what?—a gun range and angry zealots on your side?"

"Watch it," Mom says. "You're always saying I'm the intolerant one." I can't help but laugh. Oddly, Mom laughs too, as though picturing the idea herself. Her laughter is a rarity around us kids.

Not long ago, Mom went to the shooting range for the first time; she came home on an adrenaline high. "Nothing like it!" she kept repeating.

This café idea will pass. Everything does. Mom's dreams color the walls in fluid murals, and we just wait for the patterns to change. The only time Mom didn't have passion was when Allie was gone. When my sister ran away those years ago, she shook Mom's sense of equilibrium.

***

I cling to my reservations about moving out of Mom's before I graduate, but over the next few weeks Allie's forward momentum is addictive. She visits fourteen apartments, two rooming houses, and a basement rental in the suburbs. The rent seems too high everywhere, but I've decided that I'm coming with her after all, a fact Allie has taken for granted this whole time. Of course, we haven't told Mom yet, but Allie says that with no leads on a place to stay, why bother just yet?

"I'm in therapy," Allie says, out of nowhere, while we're at work. It's rare that our shifts overlap. Allie is at the register, a head cashier on management track ("I was hired with a purpose and a journey, Molly May," she'd said after getting turned down for management at the outset), and I am loading a woman's cart with cloth bags. The woman stares at Allie with a curious smile, examining her head scarf, which is adorned with penguins and stars—neither shape particularly apparent unless you're paying close attention.

"When do you have time for that?" I ask.

"Mondays, before work. It feels good to release some of the shit." She looks at the woman. "Sorry."

"Hey, no worries. Good for you, hon," the woman says as she takes her receipt. She smiles warmly at each of us before rolling her cart away. It is the first time I forget to ask a customer whether she wants help outside, and I worry she could be the mystery shopper who comes quarterly.

I haven't told Allie because I know she'll give me a hard time, but I want to move up the ranks at Swifts too. The Customer Service desk appeals to me, and the idea of selling lottery tickets and solving problems beats lugging carts in the rain any day. I've asked Rose about it a few times, and since she has seniority, she says she'll put in a good word.

"Do you talk about the attack?" I ask, as I try to catch the customer's attention with a wave as she turns the corner outside. With automated cash register stations, few customers come through our aisles, and the odds of mystery shoppers has gone up considerably.

"I talk about everything."

"Already? What have you said about me?"

"It's like a birthday wish, therapy. You can't talk about it after, not outside of that room. If you do, the spell is broken."

"Then why'd you tell me?"

"So that you know I'm doing something to get help. I know you've been worried. I was a basket case; don't act like you haven't noticed." For the first time in an hour there are no customers, so my sister turns to face me and begins straightening bags. "Your hearing is getting better, you know that? I used to have to yell."

"It's not supposed to. It's just supposed to plateau. I'm getting good at reading lips, filling in the blanks," I say. According to my doctor, I have at least 70% hearing loss in my right ear, but Allie is right that it seems better overall than when I first started exhibiting symptoms—mostly because I've learned to look for other things when communicating; hand gestures and micro-expressions. I miss the stillness of more silence, the ability to shut out half of the noise with a single earplug. Now I am attuned to the nuance of movement, which can be blaring at times.

"So. Since we have a minute. What do you say? We can make a plan to leave in one month, and we'll do it right."

"It will destroy Mom if we leave. We need to make sure she's okay."

"Nothing destroys Mom. Mom destroys herself. Believe me, Molly May, she wants us to leave."

"But Myron is getting out soon and Joey's never home. She might go insane." I pause. "The boys might go insane if we leave them with her."

"No, that's the thing. Myron can be her project. You know Mom; she always needs a project, and Myron needs to be someone's project, so it all works out. He is her son through and through. You and me ... Joey ... we are a different breed."

"That's not fair." I can tell my voice is picking up. People are staring. I breathe in through my nose and concentrate on my tone. "But what about Joey?"

"He's a possum, that kid. Nothing can destroy him. Maybe we should invite him, though. Pretty sure Joey will do his own thing wherever he goes. He's got a solid constitution."

"What about the café idea?"

Allie laughs. Not a chuckle or giggle, a full-out belly laugh that has her gasping for air, and now people are looking at her. Rose is walking toward us with a stern expression, and I put my hand up to signal that I know what she's about to say. I put my finger to my lips and stare at my sister.

A customer who carries a cart full of things in his arms approaches and drops everything on the belt with a thud. A 2-liter of off-brand cola bounces off and onto the floor. The scarf Allie has tied around her head loosens and falls around her neck as the dark, sticky liquid sprays us all.

I will have to clean this up. I grab a plastic bag and cover the bottle, running it to the breakroom sink. "We should do it. It's the one good idea Mom's had."

***

Mom returns from what was once an oddball trip to the arcade and is now her weekly trip to the gun range. She's wearing all black, cargo pants and a T-shirt, and she looks appropriately prepared for battle. It's the day we plan to break our news, and it feels like we need to do so to a woman actively trying to break bad.

I have a tablespoon of olive oil and two cloves of garlic, finely chopped, on the griddle. Collards with bacon and onions simmer in a pot next to it. Chicken and collards on a paper plate: Mom is in heaven. She only eats this meal once or twice a year, but it's her favorite, a throwback to her father's Southern-style cooking. Both of her parents were gone before I turned five, and it strikes me, as I cook, how many people Mom has lost.

"We wanted to surprise you," I say as she sniffs the air. Joey's setting the table, his headphones in and his head bobbing to the English alternative pop he seems to be into lately. The smile on Mom's face is almost beatific.

"You're making my Kryptonite. So, good news. I sold a four-hundred-dollar makeup kit to a guy at the gun range who was complaining about his wife's skin. She's going to kick his ass, but I hit my monthly target. Again."

"Mom, it's low-class to cuss so much," Allie says. I catch my brother removing one earbud to listen in. He seems to find humor in their arguments.

"It's *curse*, smartass."

"*Cuss*."

"Same fucking shit. It's low-class to have no ambition and sit around the fucking house feeling sorry for your fucking self all the time."

Joey takes off his headphones completely, nodding along with Mom, surprisingly, to which she pulls his slender frame next to her. She begins to smooth his hair as though he is a prop, and he responds by widening his eyes and tilting his head like a marionette. He walks off with arms out in front as though connected to thick strings.

Mom stares at Allie. They have the same eyes, and my sister offers a contentious reflection. But, as though remembering the meal, Mom's expression suddenly shifts.

"Get ready to be excited," she says, looking at me. I swallow audibly. Mom saying we're about to be excited never, never leads to legit excitement. It leads to heartburn and headache. It leads to officers showing up at the door, or complicated church obligations, or a new self-improvement regimen. Allie's eyes dart around the room as though she's expecting a semi to come barreling through the wall.

"Let's sit," I say, pushing on my sister's freckled shoulder. "Mom?"

"Yes, sit. So." That definitive *so* is never good either, and I suddenly feel the same sensation as I do when sitting in the dentist's chair. I imagine the drill poised above my mouth. "You might notice that your little checking account is closed, Molly May. It wasn't much, a couple hundred, but we're going to put that money to work. Together. Seeing as how I am the guardian, and you got your ear taken care of and all, I decided to make a little investment on your behalf, and you'll be pleased." I hear a sort of growling sound, and I'm unsure whether it's Cream or my stomach.

"You took my money?"

Allie stands. "We're leaving, Mom. No investment." She says it too abruptly for my comfort. I scoot toward the wall.

"We?" Mom stands too. "Leaving where?"

"Yes, we are, and none of your business. We need that money for a down payment. You can do whatever it is you're doing on your own."

Joey's mouth is an oval, and he places a cardboard-stiff hand to it melodramatically. I stare at him because he seems the safe place to stare right now, though I wonder if he's feeling anything genuine beneath the performance.

Mom's eyes are on me. Fire. I go to stand by my brother and help set the table. I notice that Joey is wearing eyeliner, and that it's expertly applied. I've tried to get that perfect line that curls up at the end of my eyes just slightly, but to no avail. He has nailed it. How can I leave him? How could I let Allie convince me that leaving is a good thing?

"You aren't leaving. Well, *you* can leave. God knows I can't stop *you* from leaving, but if you leave this time, Allie, don't come back. Ever. And Molly May is not an adult yet, so she's not going anywhere."

"I'm seventeen."

"And your seventeen-year-old ass is staying here. We're going to get rich together, and your sister can kick rocks."

"No. I'm not leaving her."

"Hey!" Joey says, then waves his hand in front of his face as though he's kidding. I'm not sure if this is self-preservation or a genuine brush-off. Can my brother really be so immune to conflict? I back away as Allie and Mom begin to yell, Mom barreling curse/cuss words her way and Allie's responses becoming ever louder and more vitriolic.

Joey follows me into the other room, where we see that Mom has brought home a brochure on how to start a café. She has papers printed from the Small Business Administration and a notepad littered with notes beneath her purse, as though she's been at a seminar recently. It's obvious that she's done her research on this one.

"That café might be a cool idea," Joey tries to interject over the yelling. He's pushing his way between them, trying to show Allie the notes. "Mom told me about it, and I'm all about life as a barista. CEOs go into that work to save their fragile hearts," he tells my sister. I try to laugh, try to ignore what is now outright screaming. We give up, and I turn off the stove.

"She cleared out my account," I tell my brother.

"Like that's a surprise," Joey says. "You do realize that Grandma used to put money in our birthday cards – why do you think the envelopes were always open?"

"Mom's freedom fund." I look around at our home, a small house with a mortgage. Everything in here is pristine, in its place, free of dust and angled to whatever Feng Shui book Mom devoured last year. Pride of ownership is what she's always saying. "It doesn't matter how little you have at first, it's how you keep it. If you respect your place, you will get opportunity. If you take it for granted, it will wither and dry up." Sometimes Mom is right.

This thought, *Sometimes Mom is right*, is what I'm thinking when I hear the shot. Joey, who is walking with me toward the living room, stops short, reaches for my hand, and squeezes. We turn, hands held, shoulder to shoulder, toward what is now a perfectly quiet kitchen. No scream, no shriek of pain. Just stillness.

***

When Myron is released, there is still a hole in the ceiling. There are boxes lined up at the door, dozens of them, and they are all precisely labeled. They don't just say "Kitchen," but rather "Kitchen, right of oven, fourth shelf. A1." Mom has been stockpiling items for months, ordering from Amazon with whatever small excess she has from her checks or makeup sales.

I pick up a box that says "Signs, equipment." It's light, and I run it out to the truck. Myron, who has been back no more than ten days and seems to have the Buddha's sense of peace now, picks up three boxes at once and trundles out as I head back in. I smile at him, but his eyes simply meet mine and he proceeds.

In less than an hour the truck is full, and all but a few boxes have been loaded. Allie is in the driver's seat wearing a blue trucker-style hat that reads "FACTS" and an eager smile. She won, and she knows it. Mom's warning shot was a sign of weakness that she can't take back. Mom is officially the unstable one.

Our new place is a small apartment above a shop that sells local art, which is above another shop where people can get piercings and tattoos. It's remarkably quiet, and Mom says nothing at all when she sees it for the first time. She helps us move.

We haul each box up three flights of stairs from the back entrance, and as we do, the creaking worries me. We have small windows that let in little light and seem clouded by either time or hardship. My sister's notebook is open on the futon we hauled up, listing all the things we need to acquire. Taking a break, I sit down on the tough cushion and thumb through the pages, which are lined with silver and cut at my fingers.

My anger was swift, low to the ground. It crept, orange-eyed and clawed. Before I had the chance to intervene, it pounced, hurling so heavy and hard that it shook my bones.

I'm reading this when Allie walks in, sweat beads covering her forehead. The day Mom pulled her gun on Allie, threatening emptily, "You shut up now, or else," years of confusion emerged. My sister knocked the gun from her hands, releasing a bullet that wove through the wood and caused Mom to fall into the cabinet. "My good dishware!" Mom screamed, and then there was another scream, a shriek, and it wasn't from pain. It was pure rage. My sister pounced, her anger leading the way, and it took only minutes before she was able to catch up and regain her sanity.

"Sorry," I said. "I don't know—"

I can't find a trace of anger on my sister's face when she catches me reading her journal. To me, Allie is transparent, herself. Instead of giving me hell for being nosy, she simply picks up where my reading leaves off. "It all came back when Mom pulled that gun. Molly May, that was our sign." I remember the chaos in the kitchen that stopped so suddenly with a shot, seeing them both reduced. Neither looked angry anymore. Instead, there was a heavy peace in the room, once it was determined that no one was hurt.

That day, Allie looked not only to me, but also to Joey, and nodded. "We're all leaving." She walked up to Mom, who was staring up at the hole, and leaned in to whisper something to her. I don't know what she said, what magic she wove, but Mom simply nodded and left the room. She's been quiet ever since.

***

Now Joey stands in the doorway, mopping his forehead with his shirtsleeve, and I'm grateful that he's here. Myron is behind him, puffing on a vape cigarette that Rattle left. I snatch it.

"Tell me what you said that day," I tell Allie.

"What do you mean?"

"What did you whisper to Mom?"

"I just told her something she needed to know about the world."

"What kind of answer is that?"

"The kind that will drive my little sister crazy," she says, a mischievous smile crossing her face.

Myron gingerly places a box that says "Downstairs. Café décor" on a fold-out table, then mutters a few obscenities under his breath. His face is still reddish, but he looks like an adult now. Juvenile correction has aged him. I think about all the violence our family has seen, and I'm not sure I want to hear Allie's answer.

Mom places her hand on my shoulder, always right behind me, but it no longer feels threatening. It is a distraction, and I close my eyes. She leans into my good ear and yells. "Mind your business, Molly May." My sister shrugs.

Mom's nails brush my cheek as she moves beyond me. Instead of punching my sister or giving us all hell for leaving her, she embraces each of us in turn. "You girls can raise the boy better than I did. You're both working; you'll be fine. No more struggling single mom with four kids bullshit for me. It works out. I'm putting the house up for sale. That neighborhood is hot. Gentrification."

"Thanks for talking about me like I'm not here. Theater, Mom. Pure theater! Can I write a play about you?" Joey asks, but Mom doesn't seem to be joking about any of it.

"If I'm going to go out of this world, I'm going to live first."

"Mom, you're a religious woman. You have to keep Myron until he's in the clear. He has community service to do."

"That's all your problem now. Fun, eh? And yes, God's will. Whatever."

Myron, who has been staring off into the distance, ambles down to the truck bed to retrieve our last two boxes. I hurry after him.

"I'm jealous," he says, when I meet him at the base of the stairs.

"Of Joey?" I ask him, gesturing to our one-bedroom above us, shuddering a bit when I imagine going up those narrow metal stairs in the snow and ice. He shakes his head.

"I'm jealous of something else. I don't even know what." He brushes off his sleeve.

"Freedom? You want to be on your own?"

"Never mind," he says.

"No. No never mind. We've barely spoken since you've been back. I want to know what's going on in your head."

"You know you yell, right?" he asks me, too loudly. I reach up for my ear, tapping around the temple to hear the echo. "Sorry, MM. Joey loves this stuff. You know he writes everything down, then teachers at school think he wrote a novel or something. All he does is write about our ridiculous lives. I can't even do that."

"You can write, Myron, I'm sure. Do you need me to read one of your essays?" He shakes his head again, lethargically, and rests the box he's carrying against the edge of the truck. "Look, I don't know what Mom's talking about, but I don't think she means half of what she says."

"Do you remember our father?" he asks.

"I barely remember Rattle," I tell him.

"Mom's dating a surgeon now, someone named Blake. She's done with church. Started chanting and collecting oils."

"Yeah. Dad feels abstract by now."

He nods quickly, as though we've both just agreed to a mutually beneficial deal. "I want to do better in school, but writing makes my hand cramp up. I *can* drive, though." The way he brushes past so many bottomless topics in a few seconds worries me.

I try to hug my brother, knowing he'll push me off, but he just stands there awkwardly, and I move his ballcap over to the side of his head, the way he used to wear it when he was a chunklet of a kid. "Hey! You don't mess with a man's ballcap. You know I've been to prison, right?" I laugh, surveying my brother, knowing that nothing I can say will change what he's been through, and he responds by putting the other box on top of the one I pick up.

"You can talk to me anytime," I tell him.

"Good. I'll take you up on that. You think Mom's going to leave me here and never come back?"

Before we can so much as chuckle over what seems an optimistic sentiment, Mom is running down the metal steps in heels, keys jangling, cursing under her breath about decisions and goals, kissing Myron on the cheek, and jumping in the truck without him. She revs the engine, then takes off.

Most of our boxes are inside and the few remaining are by the steps. We don't even question it. We play *Scrabble*, and Allie lets us drink beer, which sends my head spinning in a way I'm more used to than I'd like to admit. We toast to our crazy childhoods and argue over who gets first rights to the made-for-TV movie.

We have a somber but oddly fun time, until we realize it's night. It's the next day. We wait for Mom to return and yell or make a scene. Even Allie seems worried. We wait until we hear them. Rather, until my siblings hear them. Sunday morning, church bells. Allie is dressed for work. I have the day off. We call Mom again, again. We call our neighbor, Mr. Henry. I call Rattle, holding the receiver to my good ear. When he answers, I breathe out of my nose, slow and long, holding the moment.

"Allie? Molly May?"

"She's gone," I say.

"She's not here," he says. We both remain on the line a long time, but it feels as though we're conversing, covering the gamut, and then I hang up.

It seems like a lifetime ago. In fact, it's only been a few months, but I wait for her to appear behind me. I listen for her. I check the mail for her wild directions and plans. Nothing comes.

What does come is the realization that my family will never be whole, and when a For Sale sign is removed from Mom's front yard, we are left with no way to contact her for months.

I wait. I know I'll suddenly feel the warm breath of someone behind me. I wait for that breath.

LUCKY
Toledo, Ohio – 2019

It's not yet New Year's Eve. Grandma Dee's nails dig into the couch cushions as two men approach to introduce themselves. Her knuckles are the color of bone, her cheeks a deepening scarlet. She says, "No!" repeatedly, like a child, and the men, who wear pale blue polos that say Sacred Home Retirement Community on the sleeves, take slow steps backward with palms showing in surrender.

"I'm sorry, but we can't take her if she's not willing. That was in the agreement you signed," one of them says. He doesn't realize that my mother is incapable of reading contracts. I watch as the other man tries to lighten the mood, asking Grandma Dee about the painting of a waitress on the wall behind her. This man, whose name badge says *Tony*, has a short-cropped dark brown beard laced with red from the sun. Mom fumes, pushes both men out of her way, and grabs Grandma's arm.

"Listen, Dee, you were tough on me ever since I met your son. I respect that. Now I'm in this position to help you. I have the money to put you somewhere nice—*my money*, not your son's—and I need you to understand that it is my turn to be tough on you. For your own good."

I haven't seen my mother in action for months, and her energy surges through me, causing chills. She looks younger than I remember, even with a few flecks of silver around the temples. Giving up on the actual mothering part of motherhood must be the Fountain of Youth.

***

Mom first showed up at our apartment last night without warning, after missing my eighteenth birthday—no card, no word. After missing Myron's first A in English since he was in elementary. After missing the launch of our start-up (which was publicized in the free local paper, which we thought would surely get her attention). After missing the day that

Allie broke down in tears after therapy.

She had abandoned us physically, and, in turn, we had abandoned her mentally. She left us to our own devices, with a business idea and a small third-floor apartment. We left her to her freedom, never trying too hard to find her, allowing her to enter and leave our minds like a ghost.

I sometimes wonder if she had originally secured the apartment we live in for herself, as a place to run away to, but I never asked our landlord. Mom was tapping a savings that went deeper than I could have imagined. *Her freedom fund.*

Every month the landlord, an old man with frog-like eyes and expensive shoes, shows up to see if there are any issues with the apartment. He never asks for rent. The more we don't think about how Mom is pulling this off, the better.

Our business is no big deal—nothing to take to the bank—but it feeds us and takes care of all the other bills. It started as a mobile café with the vaguely political theme, but we discarded the political slant after one too many time-consuming arguments from customers. The concept had been a catalyst, though; it had been interesting enough to get us a few interviews and some local press. But what really took off was the mobility of the business. We couldn't afford a brick-and-mortar, so we began driving our coffee cart to bus stops and businesses alike.

It felt original, at least to the area and time. We had a food truck for coffee only, and we quickly went legit. At first, we just rolled around with a carafe, looking for those interested in a little pick-me-up with a political quote attached—whatever suited their fancy. We'd simply ask, "Red or Blue?" I felt like a drug dealer, trying to convince a group of Myron's friends, barely sixteen, that a few cups of coffee or hot chocolate would give them the energy to ace their tests. High school logic. And it worked. Soon we started getting requests from working people, college students, and kids. Our business cards went up in campus study areas and on any cork boards we could find.

The political theme is still there, under the surface, but we've settled on the name Unity Coffee, acknowledging the childishness of the quotes. Now there is only a white ring at the bottom of a purple cup. There are no holiday designs and nothing to distinguish one drink from another, aside from an *M*, *C*, or *T* for mocha, coffee, or tea. Alongside a +, ++, +-, -+ or nothing at all, for sugar, cream or any combination thereof. No soymilk, no almond milk, no rice milk. The dairy industry would be proud. Simplicity is the way we survive.

Our apartment is well-positioned, near a bagel shop with horrible coffee and a few blocks from a liberal arts college. Myron drives with the aggressiveness of a London cabbie, so he gets deliveries to people in record time. Students have ten minutes between classes, and he zooms up with caffeine and a smile, a bundle of sugar or cream in travel-size shampoo bottles that we bought in bulk online.

Allie thought Mom would be back when she saw us on the news; she was thinking that Mom would run a coup and take over the business, insisting that we put quotes from Ayn Rand on all the cups and charge more for the deliveries. "She knows we'll be successful, so she's letting us do all the hard work before she swoops in and takes over. Watch." But no. No sign of Mom that week or the next. That month or the next. Not till now.

What I want Mom to know is that we all share the tiny place amiably, but Joey is rarely home now. Myron wanders off, too, and when his school calls and Allie pretends to be Mom, she hears story after story about him being absent or walking out of class mid-lecture. He's still tortured, but he seems to be going through the motions. I want Mom to know that Allie has taken on the burdens of watching out for us. She confronts Myron, tries to get him to acknowledge his pain, and he promises to start going to school, to therapy, then he doesn't. But he shows up to work each day.

***

Mom's *Wizard of Oz* act is now up. It took a catastrophe, but she resurfaced last night to "help" Grandma Dee and jumble our collective mindset. Just as quick and silent as always, just as disruptive, she blew in and uprooted our plans and expectations. "The tornado," Allie calls her. "I knew it was coming."

Mom stood near our front door yesterday, knocking heartily, before entering with her own key. Walking past Myron, who was napping on the couch, and Cream, who mewed and tried to rub against her leg, Mom positioned herself nose to nose with Allie. No "I missed you." Just a hug,

94

a hello, then, "We need to go on a road trip."

"No," Allie said. Mom turned to me then.

"Your grandmother's sick." She spoke slowly, maybe so I could read her lips.

"What do you need us to do?" I asked, feeling something drop to my stomach. Myron and Joey needed to get started with the day's business, which made me a little nervous because, though they are efficient with deliveries, if we miss the mark on a Saturday, that could cost us our reputation. Customers are fickle. They have options.

"Fine, then, Molly May. I don't need all of you to come. How about we go, just me and you?"

"Boys, you've got tomorrow, right?" Allie asks, and my brothers nod somberly. The two of us put together a gift package for Grandma Dee and did the coffee prep for the next day to make things easier on our brothers. We closed the website to new orders and assured all those who had pre-ordered that they'd get everything on time.

We drove the familiar route earlier this morning, beyond barns and old trees, an apple butter stand and a peach farm. "How does Mom have the money to put Grandma in a home, and why does she suddenly give a shit about family?" Allie asked.

"We're adults, and she's been paying our rent."

"Maybe that pyramid scheme is working out for her. Did you see what she's driving? I know whatever she sold the house for didn't pay for that."

When we pulled up to the child-size gate that surrounds Grandma Dee's backyard, we had to park behind a BMW. Mom's BMW. We grabbed the gift bag and exchanged a glance before walking around the house to the front door. Before we knocked, however, we heard screaming, and we saw that the front door was ajar. I placed my hand on Allie's narrow shoulder as she braved first entry into the house.

***

So here we are.

"Fuck that. No. No, no, no, no, no." Grandma is rubbing her hands, looking confused and angry.

Mom is rummaging through Grandma's drawers, where she keeps

her checkbook and baggies full of change and one-dollar bills. The men make moves toward the front door. The bearded man smiles at Allie, who ignores him and follows Mom. I sit next to Grandma Dee. She's so frazzled that she barely noticed us come in.

"Sweetheart. Would you like something to drink?"

"We brought you some coffee, Grandma," I say.

"Your little business. I love it, but I'm devoted to Blend Coffee." She smiles, leans in. "Can you get your crazy mother out of here? I'm fine. I just had a few bad days."

"We'll do our best, beautiful," Allie says, reemerging and bending over to kiss Grandma. "What is this Blend?"

"Blend Coffee. My friend works there, Allie," Grandma Dee says to me.

"Molly May," I tell Grandma, wondering if I heard wrong. Her smile is childlike and distant. I haven't seen her in too long, and her eyes look like milk-soaked marbles. Her attention seems short.

Mom paces the room slowly, a lioness. I study her face and realize she looks more like the airbrushed version of her image online than she looks like she used to in real life. "Come on," she says. Suddenly forceful, she begins tugging at Grandma Dee's leg and arm.

"Mom, you can't force her," I say.

"Listen to her," my grandmother says.

"You stopped taking your pills. You could cut the blood flow to your brain by messing with those pills," Mom yells. She pulls on Grandma's arm again, and I see a redness where her fingers are. Allie pulls on Mom, and Mom stumbles back.

"You stole my pills," Grandma Dee says.

Mom brushes off her over-starched pants, rolling her eyes, having barely missed the Christmas tree that is up year-round near the front window. A cloud of dust rises, and she sneezes. I watch as she softens; she gazes at a picture, an image of herself next to my father.

Allie breaks the spell. "Grandma Dee stays here. This is her domain. We're changing the fucking locks. Why the hell call us back into your life for this? What exactly did you want us to do, shove Grandma into the car? Are we a gang now, Mom?"

"We are a family, and we are doing what's best for an aging family member. Be adults for once."

"This is adulthood? Bullying an old lady—sorry, G-ma. What's next, you going to punch us all in the faces, just to prove that filial love?"

"My neighbor has a gun. Maybe I'll go borrow it," Grandma Dee says, again, childlike. She reaches for the phone and dials a phone number, perhaps 9-1-1. When someone answers, she has enough time to say, "I could use some help over here; a crazy woman broke in," before hanging up.

Mom and Allie trade shoves like two teenage girls ready to fight over some boy. I watch them circle each other. "Fuck you, Mom," Allie says.

"Fuck me? This is what I raised? You have no moral compass, kid. You have no direction. I take care of you, and this is how you treat me? Consider that rent your own now."

"I'm the one raising *your* kids, Mom, if you want to talk about a moral compass. Paying rent on some shithole isn't enough."

"You have no idea what I sacrificed. My entire life went to you kids, setting you up for greatness, protecting you from negative energy," Mom yells.

"No. No, I'm not listening to this." Allie stumbles toward the car, and I can see her break. Her perfect face is twisted. She buckles beneath a torrent of tears, gets in the car, and doesn't even think to wait for me. She just starts the engine. A Camry races toward us and parks in front of Allie's car before she has the chance to drive away. She hesitates, watching the driver, then begins to drive away. The driver is thin, with dark hair and high cheekbones. He jumps out and walks quickly toward us.

"Is Dee okay?" he asks me at the door, confused. I shrug.

"Who are you?"

"A friend. She called me. Something about a crazy woman breaking in. That's not you, I'm assuming? Because if it is, I need to run you off."

"What are you, the comic relief?" Mom asks, but the man's comment makes me smile. He truly cares about my grandmother. I examine his face, all sharp angles and big eyes. Creases of genuine concern line his face. I say, "She's my grandmother. Pretty sure my mother here is the 'crazy' one."

"Ah. Well, I suppose I should ..." he hesitates, rightfully so, and looks over at Mom, who is standing in the doorway. "I should chat with you, then."

"Don't you think you should leave it to family?" I intervene before Mom has a chance to react.

"Not if your family's like mine," he says, leaning in close, so that I hear him perfectly. I notice that he has forgotten to remove an apron that announces him as the general manager of Blend Coffee. Unable to face whatever madness is ensuing, I cover my good ear and walk outside, along the length of the house, slowly.

I'm stuck if Allie doesn't come back, and I'm not sure what to do about Grandma. I think about calling an ambulance or the police, but the situation is too muddled to tease out. I imagine myself on the beach, allowing the sand to tickle and massage each step. A sharp breeze jolts the thought. Heel to toe, I allow the slight reverberation from the cold concrete to crawl up my legs as I move. I make my way to the backyard.

The metal fence seems so much lower than it used to, I realize, as it creaks open. I once thought this fence was impenetrable and imagined kicking it down as an officer of the law. But now it's a short thing that just needs a good nudge because the bottom digs into the dirt. I consider going into the other side of the duplex, where Grandma holds her rummage sales and paints landscapes. I consider dusting the wares, like I did as a kid, because I'm sure they need it.

A few pieces of bread are scattered around the backyard for the fat pigeons and squirrels that flock to Grandma Dee's each morning, and this makes me think that Grandma is okay after all. She hasn't sacrificed her routines. I'm wondering where the birds are today, whether I scared them off, when I hear a whimper.

The sound is persistent and gets louder as I scan the backyard; two brown eyes catch mine. Something is cowering behind a trash can. A brown dog, familiar. Perhaps the feral dog my grandmother named Lucky.

His body is thin, and his face is longer than I remember, almost wolf-like; instead of the disarming rapid pant I remember, he is breathing slowly and jaggedly. My heart surges as I take steps toward him; I remember how frightened I had been of dogs as a child, a carry-over of my mother's fear. I remember how scared I was of everything. I nudge the trash can aside and see that he's been injured, maybe run over by a car.

"It's okay, buddy," I tell him. "It'll be okay. It will."

I fumble for my cell and call Allie, who answers with bated breath. She's been crying. "I'm sorry I left, Molly May. I can't take it anymore. I love her and want her out of my life completely ... it's fucking confusing. Why is she like this?"

"I know," I say. "Come back."

I stroke Lucky's head. He has a gash across his chest; it looks as though he was dragged. His body tenses and releases with my touch. We sit together. I do not hear the man from Blend Coffee as his lips move, but I look to him and decide that he is saying something comforting and kind. His lips are a light pink and he presses them together briefly between words. I smooth down the dog's fur. I do not hear the birds or the sounds of pain or protest. I hear nothing from either ear, until my sister crouches down next to me, holding her nose. She presses her cheek to mine and whispers in my left ear.

"Molly May, I don't think we can save him. He's bleeding out. He smells." Allie examines the wound. I don't know how much time has passed, what's going on inside. I see the man from Blend Coffee staring down at me, talking to someone on the phone. "It looks infected. Don't you smell that?" Allie asks me. She's speaking slowly, as though I need help to understand words.

I feel the swell in my nose that I get before I cry, and I stuff my tears away. I imagine this dog, which I've only encountered twice, as my companion. Lucky was beaten or injured by life for no reason. As I stroke the top of his nose with my fingertips and say his name, "Lucky," his tail thumps a few times.

I realize how close my hand is to his teeth, and I realize how dangerous we all are. "I will take care of you," I whisper to him as Mom approaches. She stands next to the slender man. His mouth agape, my sister's head nodding back and forth, and my heart seizing, we all stare at Mom.

"Move, Molly May," she says. "Now!"

Grandma Dee's face is in the window and her eyes appear clear with adrenaline. I move aside. We look at each other. "We need to call someone,"

I say, but Mom is wide-legged, at attention, aiming her handgun. I stare at the brushed stainless steel, the barrel pointing toward my friend. The look on Mom's face, genuine pity, doesn't escape me. She is saving the day. In her mind, she is always saving the day.

The sound of the shot reverberates throughout my body, erasing the static in my right ear. It is louder than that day in the kitchen, and the echo creates a corporeal memory that I will never shake.

It takes less than no time for Lucky's eyes to shed their light. He is gone, just like my mother will be gone again soon, and I do not hesitate to stand up and walk inside. I sit by the tree in Grandma Dee's house, understanding everything she is feeling. Grandma Dee eases down beside me, and I smell the baby powder and rose scent of her.

"Good things are to come, kiddo," she says.

"How can you say that?"

"Because you're an adult. You're the one with freedom now." I look across the room at a pile of clothes and hats near her Christmas tree. My eyes settle on a red bulb coated in dust, then I look below to a torn package and a bejeweled hat sitting atop a pile of loud-colored blouses with everything from palm leaves to squirrels adorning them in silky repetition.

Grandma's young friend, a man I have yet to figure out, follows my gaze. I realize, in this instant, how much my grandmother needs family. How much she needs me. It's the sort of grown-up realization that twists the stomach.

Grandma kisses me on the temple and holds my head so that I can cry without making a scene. I drain myself of tears that day, not yet realizing the shift that is happening deep inside. Mom calls for help with cleanup. She is all business, and this business has distracted her from her original mission to displace Grandma Dee.

"No one's making me leave my house," Grandma Dee declares as Animal Control pulls up to the house. Mom doesn't bother scowling or arguing, just walks off with high shoulders and purpose. The man hauls Lucky to the truck bed in a sheet. Mom's beige coat is blood-splattered and covered in dirt and hair; she watches as the dog is tossed into the back of the truck.

"You did a good thing," the man from Animal Control tells Mom.

A Dodge speeds past the house with loud bass, and the man I do not know puts his arm around my shoulders as Lucky is taken away. "I take it back," he says in my ear. "Your family is worse."

At least that's what I imagine he says. All my ear feels is the warmth of his breath, his desire to be close to me. I feel my cheeks redden and wait for the rest of this day to disappear. Soon, it does. Mom does. And Allie calls my brothers to let them know we're staying with Grandma Dee for the night. Grandma Dee's friend, Vic, hands me his card before leaving. He glances over at the Christmas tree. There have been beautiful moments in this house, moments enshrined, and he looks at that tree as though it will reveal them.

***

"Grandma, what do you think about me moving in?" I ask. She ignores me.

Grandma Dee, Allie, and I sit at the kitchen table playing solitaire. The yellowing deck feels light and solid in my hands as I shuffle. I close my eyes, trying to remember my father. What I see instead is my mother, working her ass off. I see my mother, trying for so many years and being frustrated. I see my mother behind the barrel of a gun, and a growing fire spreads inside of me.

My sister makes hot chocolate and plays Grandma's jazz records, humming and tapping her fingers on the counter. She filters through a stack of mail, all of it addressed to random names, much of it looking like collection notices.

I am eighteen now, and I know enough to know that some shit is going down. I imagine our younger selves, children in the back seat of a car, whining and wondering about the world, still trusting our mother to drive us home. I do not write anything down tonight, but I resolve.

JASMINE

NOTHING WRONG
Los Angeles, California – 2029

Heavy-legged after an hour of walking, my stomach hums. I hum. My neck is leaden, weighed down by two canvas bags that were heavier this morning. It's not even 10 a.m., and I'm one True Organics™ sale away from my goal, a few sales away from folding one canvas bag and nesting it inside the other. Freedom is beautiful, a thing I will not take for granted or misunderstand again.

In the basement-level bathroom, I find an outdated but convenient fainting couch facing the sinks and mirrors. Taking a seat on the avocado cushions, I feel the first tremor and imagine my body reaching toward the ground, rooting itself, as I grip the armrest. The walls hum, the floor hums.

No sooner than it starts, the shaking ceases. The room steadies and a toilet flushes. Since I've been out, I am always aware of my position in the world, and right now I am at the base of the triangular building, near the base angle. It has been so many decades since my last geometry class, not to mention geography, but I remain a dedicated earth sign, geo-inclined. A Virgo, everyone's mother and no one's mom. No one's mom.

Rather than imagining what my children are doing right now, I do what I did inside. I begin naming U.S. capitals, as someone flushes the toilet a second time. I pause on Maine, but Augusta comes. My birthday month. So many years.

Going global is tougher. I recall global capitals inaudibly and find I can no longer remember any of the capitals in central Asia; this would be embarrassing inside. I spent so many nights committing them to memory, winning commissary every Monday afternoon trivia session.

Something is sprayed in the stall. Rather, it's spritzed, and the room smells of oranges. The woman who comes out applies grocery-store-bought lipstick instead of washing her hands, and ignores my cordial smile and gentle head nod toward the soap. When the woman rushes out, I hoist myself up and take her place at the mirror; I wipe everything down with disinfecting hand wipes and a series of prayers. Bless this sink. Some people are not worthy of my product, but everyone deserves well wishes.

The reflection staring back always seems a surprise, though not unpleasant. Not in the same way it was in my thirties and forties. My face resembles crepe paper now, and I appear to be wearing one of those awful fanny packs under my clothes. This latter observation is both disheartening and rather amusing every time, but I have never been one to dwell. I slap my lower belly a few times and stand up straight, full-on smile.

The new psychiatrist is located on the 6th floor, a floor I have yet to see. Because I spend approximately 30% of my non-working time going to appointments, making appointments, and dropping off birthday and holiday cards to doctors and staff, a new floor is a rarity. I happen to be a celebrity in most of the Med Center buildings; I know them better than I do my own mind.

To orient myself, I visualize the landscape, marker by marker. My new general practitioner is around the corner and down Whisper Curl, right next to my gynecologist and the 7-Eleven. From the base angle of the triangle, I am no more than half a block from my neurologist and allergy doctors, who share a building. My dermatologist is a mile away but right next to my dentist. I glance up at the pocked ceiling.

I remember hearing that all pyramid-shaped buildings will ultimately sink, that it's a curse carried down since ancient Egypt. The shaking returns; this time, it's just a nudge. It feels as though someone has me by the shoulders, jerking me this way and that. I close my eyes and imagine being on a boat. Jackson had always wanted a boat.

***

I splash cold water on my face before hurrying toward Suite 602. My appointment reminder chimes, and I take three flights of stairs, two steps at a time. I am a warrior. A warrior who winds herself.

Stairs are not the worst place to be in case of an earthquake, so I assume this is also true of a bombing. We read of war inside, and news reports being what they've been, it could be either. I try to remember the best practices I learned from a mandatory training all residents of the re-entry program had to attend. Stay calm, stay positive. And speaking of the memory, I sold over seven-hundred dollars' worth of product from the connections I made at that meeting. Every dollar, a part of my fund. I hoped it would be an annual event.

As I amble up the remaining flights, white-knuckling the handrail, I check my phone for reports on war. Just a war on nature, it seems.

"What a relief," I say aloud. "It's just nature."

***

The office is a different green than the fainting couch, more of a cabbage, which seems an appropriate color for a specialist. The smell of lavender is also predictable, as is the scant but tasteful décor. The walls could use a motivational quote or two. I could use a good motivational quote. This would be a good holiday or birthday gift for the doctor, so I jot a note in my phone. I still prefer paper, but my notebook is at home.

A receptionist flashes an insincere smile. "Hello, Mrs. Jasmine Anderson. You're with Dr. Alien today."

"An unfortunate name for a therapist." The receptionist is about my age but seems unfamiliar with how to form unrehearsed words, but she's good at staring. "Have you ever tried True Organics™ cosmetics? There's a blush that would complement your lovely skin. It's a beautiful shade. I'll get you a sample," I say.

"I'm allergic to makeup." The woman begins to write something. Her nametag says *Julie*. Her eyes are blue, and they waver like water, which makes me sure she is a Pisces. Water signs can be hard sells because, if they buy, they are more likely to return product half-used. Water flows, and this is a problem. Nonetheless, I persevere. I have found truth in all angles.

"Oh no, not this makeup, Julie. It's all tested for common allergens. Maybe just try and see?"

Julie doesn't smile, doesn't look up.

"Or not. I'll wait over here. No forms?"

"You completed the form online, *ma'am*. You're here to get a prescription refilled, correct?" Noting that I've been demoted to ma'am, I offer my biggest smile and shove the receptionist a free sample pack, the kind usually reserved as bonus buys or in-home parties. Julie examines it, the ingredients, then slips it in her giant purse, which is tan and seems to remain permanently open beside her. A Snickers bar peeks out, easy access. I know Julie is the type to not only wash her hands in the bathroom but likely follow it up with an antibacterial gel.

***

I don't even hear myself sometimes. I hum mindlessly and often. Jackson used to point this out, decades ago, but he has no place in my mind right now. He is a ghost. Anxious to get this prescription refilled, I begin to tally sales in my head. Income tripled when I first went on antidepressants. Sure, they make my eye twitch, but that's a minor thing when you need money.

The man next to me is reading and gives me a stare that tells me I'm doing it now, humming. The theme song to *Three's Company*. "Come and knock on my door..." just won't leave my head, so I look at the young man as I continue, nodding my head to the beat, shrugging. He doesn't seem amused.

The world feels rude today, a mouth breather with no sense of personal space. The world is a person checking a text as you tell it about your day. The world is a gum-smacking, public finger-nail-clipping misogynist. And because I know all too well that the world is just a reflection of my own thinking, I feel rather guilty about all this. I chuckle, realizing I'm still humming, and figure *fuck it*, might as well finish the song.

The television in the upper right-hand corner of the room is silent but captions explain that a young boy shot another due to a video game. My stomach curls. The next story is about a hurricane on the coast attributed to climate change. I feel electricity go up my back. I pursue the spring-line catalog to calm down. All bright pinks and corals that no one should wear, not even the red-haired model.

I once had dark auburn hair. Now it's white. I don't wear any makeup, to be honest. I don't trust the ingredients, but the car they give you when you sell and recruit enough... that car could take me places I haven't been in years. If I keep having weeks like this, then double them, and keep going a few months, maybe a year, I'll be well on my way.

"Jasmine Anderson."

I stand. The therapist in front of me wears no makeup at all, like me, which means opportunity. I see youth, a young woman who is not physically intimidated by anyone. I make a mental note to add this new doctor to the Christmas list. She needs inspirational quotes, and I will find the perfect lettering.

I go through the motions during our meeting, thinking Dr. Alien looks a lot like the therapist from *Sopranos*. Despite the impossibility of recounting a life so complex in one sitting, I run through what I can in an efficient manner. I declare myself done in a matter of minutes. I wrote my memoir in prison; we all did, and these are the takeaways.

Dr. Alien takes off her glasses and offers a tight smile. I am sure she is about to ask more about my children, but she doesn't. Instead, she makes a welcome declaration. "Mrs. Anderson, maybe you should try more of a talk therapy approach. Sometimes talking is a great release, sharing our stories and getting some objectivity."

I think about the release I felt so many years ago. A lifetime ago. But I prefer the medication. I got the prescription inside, and I'm too used to it to just start over again. I have to distract this doctor.

"This may be an odd time to bring it up, but I think my business might be of some interest to you. You have a very lovely complexion, like a freshly cracked peanut, and one of our suede brown shadows would really make those eyes pop." I lug the heavier bag onto my lap and begin digging for a sample of #432.

"You're saying I need to wear makeup?"

I can't help but like this woman. "No, not *need*. It's about augmenting what's there. It's about making your beauty shine."

"You don't wear any." Dr. Alien is the first potential client to point this out, though I have seen the thought cross more than a few faces. I notice that her shoes are the exact color of the shadow, but, more, I notice the doctor's stance. I am so grounded that it seems I am sprouting up from the very floor beneath her. "We should wean you off the SSRIs."

"Well, let me respond here. I'm old, and makeup is really made for those who are already beautiful, like you. I like my pills. They work for me. They make my mind efficient." With my gaze between two feet, I feel my insides rattle; I need this prescription.

The ground, the bookcases in the office, the chair beneath me all begin to hum like my stomach, then shake. "Maybe I should try a little makeup," I add.

"It's going to be mild, but you might want to hold on to something," Dr. Alien says.

The mild shaking quickens, then jolts. A fissure appears along the wall, and a bookcase full of self-improvement manuals falls to the ground at the same time all my makeup spills from my bag. Shadows open and foundations roll down this way and that. My business cards scatter.

As though not noticing the earthquake, Dr. Alien says, "I've seen you, you know. You make your rounds in this part of town."

"Huh?" I say. No one talks to me like that.

"You're healthy. You appear physically as healthy as anyone half your age. I bet the doctor who started you on those meds was ready to wean you off."

"Dr. Herman? No."

"I've seen you around, sitting at the round table at the coffee shop. I overheard you chatting up the baristas and regulars. You always seemed to be in a good mood, smiling and offering kind words. It is my professional opinion that you are mentally keen, too. As far as I can tell, aside from a poor choice of vocation, you're one of the most together people I have ever encountered. You just need someone to talk to, really talk to."

"My chipper demeanor is due to the medication. You can't imagine." I hear my prison voice escape me as I fall forward a bit, but I brace my knees. "I have demons, Doc." I wonder if I should tell her something real.

"How about we talk a little about your demons."

"I just need the prescription. If I had a heart condition—"

"I'm going to ask you a difficult question."

I check my phone, although no one ever calls. My only notifications are for appointments. That, and the app that tells me that my goals for the day are to reach five hundred in sales, sleep eight hours, drink eight glasses of water, write four-thousand words, go to an audition for a laxative commercial that I saw advertised on Craigslist... "You're on a really high dose, and this medication is relatively new."

I am never irritated, not anymore. Life is too short. But I am stumped. Doctors are some of the nicest people I know. Doctors never talk down prescriptions. Mental illness is a real thing; antidepressants help people. Dr. Alien needs to understand. Or be replaced.

The doctor begins picking up my makeup and cards, including my parole officer's card. She gives it an extended glance, then makes neat piles and packs the canvas bag like a pro. "I'd like to chat with you more."

I am trying to find calm, reciting the periodic table from upper left to lower right in my mind. So many hacks in the world. "Why aren't you fazed by the quake?"

"Why aren't you?"

"I suppose you get to ask the questions." Now I hear the confrontation in my own voice. This is the old Jasmine, the Jasmine who had yet to be rehabilitated by the State of California in partnership with the State of Ohio.

The quivering returns as Dr. Alien maintains eye contact with me. She has lovely eyes, doesn't even need mascara.

The shaking turns violent, and I struggle to stay upright. We need to get to the desk, where nothing blunt can hit us in the head. Books fall at an angle. I remember teasing out the Pythagorean theorem, that the longest line to fit inside a cube must be diagonal. The way items shift in this room is inefficient. Nature cannot be efficient in this building.

We crouch down, crawling out of the office like cats—low to the ground. We find ourselves alongside Julie and the man who'd been annoyed by my humming. The man is clutching a historical novel to his chest as though it is a child. An air sign.

Two earths, an air, and a water under a desk. The fire surrounds us.

The earth itself is breaking beneath our weight, and we huddle near each other like a pack. My mind is as rattled as my body.

Julie takes a bite of her Snickers, shoves the rest of it in her mouth. The doctor's palms are flat to the earth and her head hangs over crossed legs. I mirror this pose. I am flexible, thanks to seven years of daily stretching.

Dr. Alien, despite the earthquake, the location, and the fact that others are around, continues from her coiled-up position. "I hope you understand what I was saying. You are not broken."

"With any luck, none of us are." Air.

"We'll be fine. I think." Water.

"I will happily buy that eye shadow. I will happily buy the shadow because it's a perfect color for me, and I think this too will pass."

I try to remember geology class, a subject I found difficult because, though the connection was there, there was so much space between me and the inner core that I figured it'd never matter. I also remember a mumbling instructor. I had memorized the layers beneath the crust but never gave them enough thought to allow the information to permeate my long-term memory.

"I spent most of the last decade in prison because I failed at motherhood," Jasmine says. "Happy? You still want to take me on?"

Dr. Alien, curled over her legs, looks up and says, "I'll refill your prescription once, yes, but I want to hear more."

There are other doctors who can supply prescriptions, hundreds of them within a square mile who wouldn't bat an eye at a request for a common medication and wouldn't pry—these doctors understand that the blurring of reality is necessary in so many minds—but this one is different. Ignoring the persistent eyes of the young man nearby, I calculate the shadow at twenty-four dollars and realize I've made my goal for the day. I enter the number in my phone and smile at the ding. For a moment, I think of the kids.

Fissures appear at the building's seams and work their way up. Another pyramid sinking toward the ground. Dr. Alien and I exchange a look of knowing, waiting it out. The ground beneath us hums, but the earth won't shatter. Not yet. I wonder if I should talk to someone.

MOLLY MAY

RECKONING
The Road – 2020

Transparency is the reason my generation is so self-conscious. There is nowhere to hide, except behind avatars, which I refuse to do. I scroll, ignoring the political ads, longing for a time I could look something up without a barrage of emotive ads interrupting me.

Election season is contentious in Ohio; people argue in grocery lines and bookstores about what it will take to collectively heal the underlying issues with our economy and calm the social ire. The number of mass shootings and riots in response to abuse is rising. I minimize a large donation ad. I minimize any "Breaking News" because reading isn't enough.

I look for Mom's image online. The version of my mother that Lee's Mature Fashions chose to keep is thinner, has red hair, and unnaturally green eyes that are wider than I remember. This version of Mom appears both scared and surprised. There are no wrinkles or blemishes, no signs of life. She is relegated to the swimsuits and dumb stares that accompany retail.

I am still staring at this image when I call Grandma Dee, who sounds better each day we speak. "Ms. Molly May. My favorite grandchild. Don't tell the others," she says. She says this to all of us.

"Hi, Grandma. Do you feel as good as you sound?" I notice that not only is her voice fuller, but she sounds giddy, as though she's hiding something.

"Your mother hasn't been back to harass me yet, but I'm ready if she shows up. I'm studying Tae Kwon Do." She laughs. "Bruce Lee invented it. I found some money in an envelope. My mother told me that if you find money, you need to spend it."

I'm pretty sure she's wrong about Tae Kwon Do, but I keep that to myself. "They teach a lot more than art at the community center now? How much money?"

"It's either that or Zumba. I've taken everything else," she says. "That Sacred Community place scared the piss out of me, and a couple thousand. I think it must have been your grandfather's stash." *Mom.*

Grandma Dee sounds good today, stronger. I can't get a word in. I'm about to try, when she adds, "You know, Molly May, my young friend Vic would like to speak to you again. He asks about you every time I see him at the coffee shop. I think you made quite an impression."

"Yeah?"

"That boy seemed devoid of emotions before he met you. I think he's been really hurt. Now he's all smiles and sweetness. It's sickening." I can hear the mirth in her voice.

I hold the phone tight to my left ear. "Maybe one day," I say. I imagine Vic, serious eyes that hint at a story I am curious to know. I'm baffled that he'd want anything to do with our family after that day, so I ask, "But are you sure?"

"Can I give him your phone number?"

"Sure." I say it a little too urgently. I don't have time to care about this man.

"Good, because I already did. Maybe you'll fall in love and move to Toledo. It wouldn't be so bad to have some family around here."

"You might be onto something," I tell her.

"Tell me about you," she says.

Allie, my brothers, and I—we feel the full weight of running a small business while two key employees are still in high school. The problem is that demand is increasing, and we *do* have to pay rent ourselves now. Mom's savings account is questionable, and credit card bills in her name are showing up regularly. Allie is writing *Return to Sender* in the thick black Sharpie we use to date product. If only we knew where to forward these letters. Mom's going to be in deep shit if they catch up with her, Allie always says. "Not much going on, Grandma. We're working a lot, trying to ignore the news."

"I hope this chaos settles down. Feels like there's a new controversy every day," Grandma Dee says with a sigh. I can hear her TV over the phone. She recounts everything she hears, with commentary, and I interrupt her monologue.

"Can't wait to see you," I tell her.

"Oh, I bet you can't wait. I don't know if it'll be to see *me*, though. I heard your voice change when I brought up my friend Vic. Tell the boys hello. I love them, but I know they won't call. Tell Joey to send me more clips of his show. That kid's going to be famous." Her voice gets pitchy when she says famous, as though to emphasize, and I laugh. "I know that sister of yours won't come, so tell her thanks. I love you all."

The boys are rarely around to speak with Grandma Dee on the phone. Phone calls seem an archaic form of communication to them. I'm glad that Grandma Dee is spared, though. I wouldn't want her to worry. Myron keeps threatening to go into the military, and his latest choice in a girlfriend—the lead singer of a heavy metal band—pulls him away to gigs whenever he's not working. He drinks too much cheap beer but still delivers our shipments on time. Joey constantly offers up threats to move out because "this space is depressingly small, and this town is oppressively simple," and it's only a matter of time. "New York, here I come!" He's in one show after another, a rising Instagram and YouTube star who checks his followers and playbacks every hour, like clockwork.

"You do realize that if everyone is famous, then no one is," I once said, and he stormed out without so much as a joke.

***

When I go to see Grandma Dee, I am solo. I take Allie's car without too much protest on her part. Instead of accusing me of slowing down business, Allie seems happy and a bit curious about Vic. I'm oddly nervous as I drive. I feel as though I'm driving toward a newly shaped world that has yet to reveal itself. When I arrive, Grandma Dee is sleeping, but she has left the back door open. Anyone or anything could have walked in.

I kiss her on the cheek, and her eyebrows crinkle. She licks her lips and bats her eyes open. "Hey, kiddo. I'm getting up."

"No need," I tell her, turning off the lights of her Christmas tree to dim the room. "I'll be here a few hours. I'll keep myself busy. I'm locking the door, though."

"You could clean the basement if you get bored," she says, chuckling,

117

and I set out to do just that. Grandma's pink housecoat looks warm, but I put a throw blanket near enough that she can grab it if she wants. "Just a catnap," she mumbles, and is asleep sooner than I can get out of the room.

Grandma Dee's basement used to be off-limits, a trove of possibility. Now half is filled with bomb shelter-worthy fare and the other half is filled with memorabilia—all of it settling beneath a blanket of sticky dust. I have a bundle of cloth rags that Grandma Dee makes from old clothes and a bucket of soapy water because rag and spray alone won't budge this dust.

When I begin to wipe down the shelves, the air fills with particulates, and I search around for a mask and gloves, which I'm sure exist but are likely below a coating of dust as well. Somewhere below the muck I find a few picture frames, small ovals with awkwardly cut photos inside. One frame contains my parents, who are stilled by time and, judging from Mom's bangs, hairspray. Another depicts a young boy at Halloween, who is dressed up like a ghost and doing his best haunted-eye look. I see a smile behind his intent to look scary and stern. I turn the pic to see my father's name, Jackson, and a little note that says "Second choice of costume. Baseball player next year."

My father is about Myron's age in this photo, the age Josh was when he cashed his life in for points. I place both images on a stand that has been cleared of dust. Holding my breath, I find more of my father's old books. *The Hardy Boys* and *The Cave of Time,* a Choose Your Own Adventure book that I set aside to read that night.

By the time I go back upstairs, I have an armful of family history, and Grandma Dee has turned on her holiday lights again. It's nowhere near Christmas time, but she's dedicated to the season. I sometimes wonder what her neighbors must think. She's making cinnamon tea, and when she turns and sees me with two armfuls of items, she shakes her head. "You always wanted to pick things out. Can't just do the job." I see a slight upward turn of her lip.

Grandma Dee curls her short hair and wears pale lipsticks that range from the exact color of her face to the color of a summer peach. Her lipsticks are lined up in the bathroom in a rainbow of beige to light brown. Lipstick is the only makeup she wears, aside from mascara on special occasions.

"I made pretty good progress," I say. "I may have to spend the night if you want me to finish. I mean, if Allie lets me keep the car."

"You dusted everything?"

"I got most of it. I dusted the canned goods. I don't think all those green beans are still good, Grandma."

"Those green beans will kill a small cat!" she says, and I see both edges of her lips tilt up. Seeing that her energy is back, I offer to make dinner if she'll tell me a story about my father, and without pause, she launches into it. I watch her hands move as she animates her words.

"Your father loved dogs, Halloween and motorcycles. Oh, and scaring me! He'd bring in these garter snakes from the yard, which were just about the early death of me. Speaking of things, do you know anyone named Blake Jonson? He's getting a lot of bills. I opened a few, and I have a feeling someone will be coming after his ass if he doesn't pay up soon." Her words are large, but her movements are small, and this is all I can think as I try to place the name. I remember a man in a Jeep dropping Mom off one day, a doctor.

"Don't open any more. I'll take them back to the post office," I say.

***

I get a speeding ticket on the way home, and swallow hard when I hand it to my sister. "I'll pay it," I say.

"At least you don't want to be a cop anymore," Allie says flippantly. "If you did, I'd be on an island here."

"I'm still going to the Academy. I'm ready." I deepen my voice. "Grandma Dee says to call her. She loves you."

She looks away. "Yeah, yeah. I will."

Sun Ra songs play on repeat; a retro record player that Allie picked up at a thrift store sits on the windowsill. It's cold outside, but the sun is magnified. Not long ago, Joey positioned a mirror at an angle so that the sun would reach us in the living room and provide him a sort-of spotlight to practice in and shoot his short audition videos. This is also where we do most of our packaging in the winter because it's warm.

I wish he were here right now to help, but the wish is selfish. We need the manpower. I have four pounds of espresso beans to package in small brown bags with decorative yarns, and my hands are dry. The scratchy yarn makes my teeth itch. After an hour, I give up on the yarn and just package all the beans. Joey can take care of the rest when he comes back.

I willfully ignore the thoughts that weave in and out of my head as Allie plugs the sales numbers into an Excel spreadsheet that we update at the end of each day. Thoughts of Toledo, of Mom, of war. None of it new. All of it too much. The credit card bills coming to Mom worry me, and I set out to keep the next one. I need to find out how much she owes. It may be that debt, not us kids, that's keeping her away. As bittersweet as this thought is, it sends warmth down my arms.

"We hit our target," Allie says, hitting return a final time before closing the Profit and Loss statement. My sister is a brilliant manager, if a bit micro-focused, and I am a brilliant salesperson—if I do say so myself. We are the perfect team. Then again, coffee sells itself. "I think it might be time to hire someone." She rubs her hands together vigorously.

"Good. I can't keep up," I say. *Mom would be proud*, I think.

My sister is all in, and the only time she really takes for herself is a weekly session of therapy that seems to be helping her confront the ghosts. She has reconnected with old friends, many of whom tracked her down online or through the business. She had disappeared from her old life, too beaten down to advocate for what she believes, and we would sometimes accuse her of having never been part of a movement at all. "You were probably just living with some guy who bought you pretty things," Joey would say from a safe distance across the room, and my sister would chase him out of the house. I know that Allie's drive is still there—it's not all tied up in the business. I know it because I see the fire blazing behind her eyes when she listens to music or watches the news. She is strategizing.

What worries me about my sister are her whiteboards, and the sense I get that she is about to use our company as a platform for something bigger than we're ready to take on. Her plans are everywhere, but her intent is myopic. She forgets us, forgets Grandma. She's too busy saving the world. Goals and action items are listed on whiteboard paint in the bathroom and living room, and on chalkboard paint in the kitchen. Our rooms are filled with plans coded by acronyms that she's read in business books at Barnes & Noble.

She wants us to live and breathe the business, outside of school in my brothers' cases. In our latest SWOT analysis session (no, I'm not kidding), Allie says our weakness is online marketing, and I stare at her for a long time, just to see if she'll acknowledge what I am thinking, because I know she can read my mind. A woman obsessed, a carbon copy of her mother, only the inverse.

"There's a women's rights protest in Chicago next week. I was thinking we could provide free coffee. We have a platform now, so let's back protests and voter-education seminars. Ramp up the online outreach!" She claps, laughs at our somber expressions, and pours a short glass of white wine to celebrate her P&Ls. "We need to get back to our roots. This isn't about party lines anymore. It's about education. Change."

I block off my good ear, listening to an audiobook about the history of coffee. I post a few images, black and whites, of coffee cups held gracefully, trying to ignore the sneaking thoughts of Vic. I post sepia images of grounds and espresso machines. I post images of us, the home, the boys, but I crop out all the dingy stuff. I raise my fist to the sky and hit *Send*.

***

Though she has a key, I'm pretty sure, when Mom returns, she knocks gently. School is about to begin again for my brothers after winter break, and Allie asks if I hear the door.

I have a single earbud in most of the day, too, but no music threading through it. I read somewhere that by cutting off the good ear, I may be able to improve capacity in the bad one. People do this with vision and eye patches, too, but I have a feeling my efforts will prove futile.

The last time I see our mother, she is wearing fur. A fur-lined coat, fur-lined boots, and a fur muff. She's gained weight but looks good. In fact, she looks divinely outdated, as though she walked off the set of a black-and-white film. She tells us we're on our own now and hands us a drive that contains receipts for all the rent she's paid. "I spent the last twenty years of my life raising four kids on my own, and now I'm done." She hands me her key, and when I take it, her small, cool hand grips mine for an extended moment before she releases.

"Life is like a string," she explains, sitting on the couch next to Myron. "You stretch it, and really look, and you can see how much you have left.

121

We only get so much time. I don't think I have a lot, so I'm going to do what the fuck I want."

We just stare, Joey and I, from the floor, where we do much of our packaging work every day on a tarp. We continue to work as the madness commences, figuring this is just another dramatic scene, perhaps one of the first monologues. We don't realize it's Mom's last.

"Poetic, Mom. We're grown. We got this," Allie says. She seems oddly stoic.

"Your grandmother has a space reserved at Shady Creek Retirement. It's a better retirement home, stronger caretakers, more cooperative staff. Here's the card. I need you to contact this lawyer, and after he has you sign a few forms, you give this accountant your account information, and you'll be set for a while. Don't get lazy, though."

"What in the holy fuck, Mom?" Myron says.

"You all do your resolutions?" she asks, then catches herself. "Never mind, never mind. Work on yourselves. With our genes, you all are halfway through life, especially you boys. The men in our family die young and loud." She looks at Allie. "I'm almost done. I just wanted to say goodbye and make sure you are taken care of. Say what you want, I always took care of you."

"Is this supposed to be a cry for help, Mom? Do you need help?" My sister's face has become my mother's, I realize, and the worry—all the unknowns that torture the protectors—has been transferred. My mother is the one who can run away now.

"No, Allie. I'm not going to kill myself. Fucking get real. God loves me too much for that. What does God have planned for you? That's the question. I've done all I can to help." She leans in to whisper something in Allie's ear, and the two of them stand there for a long time. I can make out *I'll take care of it*, but I'm not sure of what. Mom then hands both Allie and me small cards that say "Everything is an experiment." She leaves two additional cards near my brothers.

We all wait for a swollen moment, and then Allie leaves the room.

Mom looks at Myron. "I'm not leaving you. This isn't just some midlife crisis. I hope you'll gain a little empathy as you grow into your own, but whether you do or don't, just know I did my best. I tried to make you strong, and I had a lot of shit going against me. I have one more thing to do; then I'm leaving this fucking country."

"What happened to America First?" Allie yells from the kitchen.

"I have a shipment to deliver," Joey says. He grabs a few cups and a few bags and packs them deliberately before rushing off. He doesn't look back at Mom, will never see her again. Myron just continues to stare, a barreling train in his eyes.

"I'll leave you all be. Please do not try to contact me." She looks to Allie. "I put in an anonymous tip, too. Sue those assholes."

"This isn't some fucking movie, Mom," Allie yells. "Don't do it."

But it feels like a movie. Our life has been a series of clips ever since I was a kid. Full of drama and long pauses in time, we simply fill in the liminal space and wait for the explosions. Mom walks out the door and down the metal stairs in her heeled boots. The world turns black and white, and I watch as she throws her scarf over one shoulder. She gets into a new and unfamiliar black car, a rental probably, and drives off as soundlessly as she arrived.

"Mom!" I call. I want to ask her about the credit card bills, but she does it again—pulls some cheap shit from a movie and blows me a kiss.

***

That's it. After she's gone, I can't stretch out the scene in my mind or make it more romantic. My sister kicks the wall hard, creating a gaping hole in our apartment wall. Mom just came, handed us a self-help mantra, some bullshit instructions, and left. No hugs, no tears.

Over the next few weeks and months, nothing. We check in with Rattle; rather, I do, and he hasn't seen her; Grandma Dee hasn't seen her, and no one at any of her previous jobs has heard from her or so much as glimpsed her around the way. When we call the lawyer's number, a man says he has no idea who we are or what we're talking about. When we call the accountant, he says he is a retired veterinarian who helps people out with their taxes, and that he drops his business cards in any fishbowl that promises the potential of a free meal. I tell him I like his style and will call him back around tax time.

***

"I don't really talk to anyone about this, and I feel like I'm unloading

123

on you," I tell Vic. His eyes brighten before he tells me, "You know, if it makes you feel better, I can share some of my family craziness. My parents used to iron all my clothes. Socks, underwear ... my father ironed my sheets. Just to give you a glimpse into my shit show of a family life."

"We have a lot to learn," I say, imagining him next to me on the couch.

Vic and I speak on the phone for hours. The first person outside of family who shares that intangible thing, that thing where we anticipate each other's needs and say what needs to be said. I begin making pilgrimages to Grandma Dee's to check in and, selfishly, to get together with Vic. Allie just nods her head. "Going back to Toledo?"

"Mmhm."

"He's older. If he's not married, go for it. Better yet, enlist him. He works for that chain, right? Let's pull him over to our side. We need some feet on the ground in the Northwest," she says.

"Allie, if I leave, will you tell me what you and Mom whispered about that day?"

"I told her the truth about what happened. I told her he raped me, and she said she knew. She said she had failed."

I wait for her to say more, and, as expected, she walks over to the speakers and turns the dial to *High*. Carlos Santana and John Lee Hooker take over the apartment, filling it with possibility. I may or may not hear them totally, but I feel the music in a new way.

***

It doesn't take me long to do exactly as I'm told. I enlist my crush. We date, we partner. Vic and I go to the movies, like I imagine ordinary people do, and he's considerate enough to sit up front, near the speakers. We eat Italian food and laugh and exchange stories about our childhoods that could put any memoir to shame. He's loud, and he loves the fact that I can't hear as well as most people, because he says he gets complaints about his laugh. "People say it's annoying, that I need to use my indoor voice, but you'll never know." His smile is thin and wide, a gift.

"I kind of do know," I tell him. "I mean, you're really loud." I watch his hesitant smile.

"Honestly, I never laughed much before anyway," he tells me.

We are a love story, too sappy to dwell on; we are, if not movie-worthy, soap-opera worthy, as we watch a matinee. It's a day we both should be working. Allie will call to give me hell later about being gone so long, but I don't care. The movie is sad, about a woman with a brain tumor and the love of her life; in one of the final scenes, the woman, who is rail-thin, says, "My life is like a string. It seems I could have forever left, but when I stretch it, I can see that I'm almost to the end." She extends her hands and pinches her fingers together to signify what she has left, just as my mother had. The rest of the movie is a series of clips of her doing the things she's put off. I imagine my mother doing the same.

When we walk out of the theater, I ask him if he's ever heard the string analogy before.

"No, and you'd think they would come up with something better than that."

"Really," I agree. "Is this movie really just out? Is it a remake?" Just as I ask, I get a text from Grandma. "It was nice having you here." There's an image that is probably supposed to be an emoji but just translates as an empty box. Just as I turn my phone light off, I get a follow-up text. "I got another one of those bills for Blake Jonson." And my mother's face stretches to something Daliesque in my mind.

Vic shuffles his feet and takes a step back from me. "Molly May, listen. This is serious. My ex is being difficult. She won't sign the papers, so we're technically still separated. The process is just tougher than I imagined. I haven't told you because …"

I nod, still thinking about my mother, the black-and-white movie version distorting in my mind, saying something so fortuitous and strange. Perhaps it is just a saying, but it dawns on me now that it doesn't matter. I can't help but think my mother is sneaking up on me again, catching me off-guard, trying to use her family for everything she can. "You're fine," I say to Vic, meaning it, meaning that his baggage is the least of my worries. He's perfect to me.

Nonetheless, annoyance creases Vic's forehead; he says nothing. "Did you hear me?" He wants drama, and I refuse.

"I heard you. Divorce isn't finalized. I don't want to be involved, but I understand," I say. We part awkwardly, with a mindless peck on the lips and a see-you-soon. I am eager to get home, and I ride the gas too heavily for two hours, beyond cornfields and cows, beyond everything still and ignored about Ohio.

My siblings are asleep when I arrive, and I place a blanket over my computer so the glare won't wake Joey, who is snoring on the couch, still in his jeans. He's the light sleeper in the family, and I type slowly in my fort of technological glare.

A text comes in. "You made it home safely?"

"Yeah, Vic. Thanks. Lots on my mind tonight."

"You sure you're not upset?"

"Yes! I have family issues on my mind." I want to tell him that I don't have the space in my head for more issues, to even be angry or worried about something I know he'll take care of. The one part of my life that seems to flow is our relationship. How do you write things like this in a text? I don't even try.

I let him go to sleep worried, unsure how to interpret my response. It's hard to tell him how much I trust him. I probably seem cold and uncaring, but his divorce is something I can't worry about. There are parts of life that I just know are right. Then there are the mysteries, the all-out fuckeries. My mother's words are what haunt me now—overwhelming my thoughts, stealing my sleep—and *she* worries me, not a man who I trust is trying to move on.

The next morning, I feel a wave of cold. My sister moves the blanket with flourish, smiling down. "Have fun? I'm surprised to see you back."

I have not slept, and my computer screen is full of writing, a still of my haphazard thoughts. On the verge of change, thoughts become messy and fast, a series of fragments that one can only hope will solidify. *I often wonder if insanity means getting caught in the middle of change, getting caught in the resistance.* I delete that sentence, then close out the page without saving. The fragments are released.

"Seeing Mom was like seeing a ghost," I say, groggy but still too loud, waking my brother.

"Huh? She really shouldn't be there," Allie says.

The two of them wait for me to explain. I can't, not yet. "She wasn't there long. I think she's finally gone for good." A few days will have to pass before they stop pressing me. And soon I realize how right I am. The bills continue to come, and with each one, we all know that Mom is farther away.

***

My brothers and Allie are making a mail-order dinner a month later, reading the instructions to each other and awkwardly chopping veggies. The result is supposed to be a healthy version of enchiladas and cauliflower rice, but these meals often go sideways, and we end up throwing all the ingredients into a slow cooker. I set the table, not quite sure yet how to break the news—the change that is coming. "How about we open a bottle of wine?" I say. I will be heading to Toledo again, for the sixth time since I last saw Mom, the next day. Every time I see Vic feels like a cause for celebration, but this weekend we will go out in style.

"Beer," Myron says, opening a new one as he downs the rest of a can. He's wearing a black shirt that has his girlfriend's band name across the back. The Dinosaurs. His belly hangs out the bottom slightly, and I tug at the shirt.

"You look like a forty-year-old man."

Joey laughs. He moves his shoulders back, standing arms toward the sky, superhero-style, as he stares at me. "This can't be good. What are you about to tell us?" He looks down at *my* stomach. "You have been spending a lot of time in Toledo with that guy."

I don't humor him. "Close," I say. "I want to launch our business in Toledo." I realize the wine is not open, and I haven't even waited for everyone to sit. My brother fumbles to open and pour the wine fast, scooting a glass my way, as Etta James Live begins to thread through the speakers and into the right hemisphere of my brain.

"Toledo, Ohio?"

"We need to take care of Grandma Dee, but she doesn't want to leave her duplex, so I was thinking I could move in. I ran the idea by her, and she seems thrilled."

"She'll be a pain in the ass," Myron says. He pushes the wine glass that Joey placed in front of him my way. I take it but do not drink. Meanwhile, the one direction I haven't yet been able to look—at my sister—beckons. Heavy-necked, I look over at Allie, who has spatula in hand and doesn't miss a beat. She dresses the plates with sour cream and salsa. "Grandma lives near the university, and she needs you, girlie. It'll be a good move. But promise me you're not moving for a married man."

"He's getting a divorce finally, and no. He's a part of the formula but not the reason."

She smiles, flits her hand in the air. "Go on, then."

"Won't you miss me?"

"Ha! Won't I? You're killing me, but it's just a two-hour drive."

"Yeah, the way you drive," Joey says.

"We'll be okay." Allie downs an entire glass of wine and pours another. I glance down at the crimson liquid. The bottle is almost empty already, and I push my glass back across the table as she rushes to the nearest whiteboard, erasing some marketing targets and jotting notes about Toledo. She draws a makeshift map of the college there, and its proximity to Grandma's house, doing a few calculations about gas and drawing stick figures for the two people she thinks we should hire. "Get students. They'll work as cheaply as these guys." She points to our brothers. "You can launch our online presence. I mean, we're barely visible online. Maybe you could take care of orders."

"I'm not sure if I can do this alone, but maybe Vic can help."

"I bet he can," Allie says with a smirk, reaching for my wine. "I'm going to have to go with you to launch the business. You boys got the homefront for a few days, right?"

While Grandma Dee's neighborhood will not soon see revitalization, the bones are there, and the location is good. Joey's HGTV habit, coupled with a nearby Lowe's, gives us ideas for the house, which Grandma Dee says she'll consider. When I tell her I'm finally moving in, she says, "Honey, you don't tell a person you're moving in with them. You ask them, and you hope they say yes."

"Grandma Dee, may I move in with you?"

"Yeah, why not?" Her self-amused laughter is loud enough that I move the phone to my right ear for silence, relief.

We move my few backpacks' worth of stuff and no more than four boxes, minimalism being a mainstay of our sibling household these past years. Grandma Dee is doing something I never see her do as we wave goodbye to Joey and Myron—she's not trying to hide her smile. She stands on the porch, arms outstretched, and embraces both of us. "You girls don't realize how much this means to me. I feel whole again." She grabs my chin. "But you'll have to earn your keep around here."

Allie takes us both by the shoulders, trying to ignore a man walking down the street muttering to himself as she jokes off what I know to be true. "Grandma Dee, we might have to be the ones to put *you* to work."

As we lay out our plans, Grandma Dee tells me stories about my father when he was a kid, and he sounds like the perfect combination of Joey and Myron, who will likely be moving out to their respective posts in life soon. Joey has a job with a small theater now, but he's saving, and Myron is full-time for Allie, who's a manager at Swifts now and hires punk kids his girlfriend knows to do deliveries; then gets furious when they call in due to hangovers.

***

Allie, on Mom's recommendation, sans lawyer, sues the police department Griffin worked for, and she presses charges for the attack, bolstered by the tip that sparks the police investigation; the #MeToo phenomenon that carries many women from the shadows of abuse returns with Allie's case, and I long to be back by her side.

Some of her old comrades, people I thought didn't truly exist, begin to show up at the apartment and contribute to her whiteboards and strategies about how to expand knowledge, when I come back home weekends to catch up. Some agree to testify; others explain, shakily, that they just can't. A man is convicted, and it comes out (not to me, but on the news) that Allie was initially confronted by another man.

"Too much drama right now, with all I have going on," a girl in a pink "Eat this!" T-shirt tells a newscaster. It is after I watch this that I open a new computer window and begin to take practice police exams. I dive into these study guides for weeks, losing myself in the psychological standards and purposely not looking up physical restrictions.

By New Year's Eve, I imagine Mom dusting off her palms, claiming the case was only possible because of her impetus. It is this time of year that I always think she may sneak up behind us all.

Mom had saved the day by calling the police in the first place, submitting that tip—which I'd find out much later was delivered by the man who had found Allie. Still, I imagine Mom by his side, dialing the number and placing the phone to his ear. I will never stop imagining that she is taking care of us in her own twisted, controlling way.

Just as I imagine Mom, however, I realize this will be the first holiday season without her, and my fantasy fades. I am knitting with Grandma Dee on the couch as a light snow begins to fall. I don't hear my phone, and when I look down, I find over a dozen texts. I begin to scroll, thinking they must be notifications that my sister is on television, but instead they are all SOS calls from Myron, who never texts me. A single text from Joey says "Get home now. We need you now. Now!"

"I'll call later," I yell, as I press the *Call* button on Joey's name. Grandma Dee and Vic call after me, inquiring, but the urgency pulls me out the door and into my car. Joey answers on the first ring.

"Finally. Come home, Molly May. I can't tell you what happened because you won't be able to drive. Just get here, and we'll figure things out."

"I'm in the car. Is it Allie? What'd she do?"

"It's worse than that. Come here."

Time limps along as I drive beyond bare trees and piles of lumber. I don't encounter any bad traffic, any traffic at all, in fact, but I do feel heat building up inside as I drive. Whatever happened, its timing sucks. I am finally happy, driven enough to follow my own heart. I am ready to build a life for myself, and whatever crazy thing this is will undoubtedly unravel it. All the selfish thoughts circling in my head collide as I press on the gas too heavily.

Twelve stop lights from Columbus, I navigate the long stretches of country road, passing the dairy farm and the apple butter stand. All of it looks different now. I remember that I used to imagine working at the apple butter stand, crushing apples with my feet like Lucy did in an old black-and-white episode of *I Love Lucy* that Mom and I watched. I'm coming from the opposite direction, heading to Columbus rather than returning. I speed up after a few miles, searching for the gray house that sits on the corner near a fork that tells me I'm almost to the last light. Miles give way, and I see it at last. Satellite radio plays quiet dance music, a station Joey set, and I never bothered to change. I hit another button and find jazz. My sister's pick, no doubt. I hit another and find rock. Two more rock stations, and I settle on old-school hip hop, which usually makes me smile.

I don't realize how fast I'm going until I see them, blurred and angry—red and blue lights muddled slightly by the fat snowflakes that have fallen on my windshield. I don't hear the siren, only a whoop. Only a blip. This car is under Allie's name, and though I've received speeding tickets on this route a few times now, I know that this will be something more complicated.

My body swells as I wait. No officer gets out of the car for a long time, and I'm sure they're running the plates as I wait. Maybe calling for backup. I see a signal from a female officer, a finger up as if to say "just a minute." I turn on my phone and begin to read the news.

"Dozens of protesters were picketing outside of Precinct 4 when it happened. As soon as the news broke, a counter-protest began, and things began to get violent." A Blue Lives Matter sign flashes, and I feel as though I am about to throw up. As I read on, I find my sister's attacker smiling at the camera with his brother. The two of them hold fishing poles and look like the nicest people in the world. "Unidentified woman shoots Columbus police officer Griffin Yates. One bullet is still lodged in the officer's hip, reports say. The suspect is still at large."

Protesters. I glance in the rearview and see the officer heading toward my window. She is a stern-looking woman with big eyes, and she simply stands. I roll my window down, and she motions for me to open the door and step out. My body is rigid. Every movement feels laborious. Given the contention between my family and the police, it is possible that this woman has my name on a list. She could pull a gun or arrest me, make claims that I'd resisted or had drugs in the car. As I watch her move, shoulders square and mouth straight, I imagine myself in her position. The cool air fills my nostrils, and my eyes begin to water as the wind hits, the way they always do this time of year.

"You were speeding," she says. She looks at me for a long time. "Again."

I recognize her. She pulled me over once before, shortly after I moved. "I'm very sorry. I have my license and all. This is my sister's car, but I can

… I was rushing for a reason."

"I just want you to be careful. I will write you a ticket because that's my job, but we do it electronically now, so I just need to swipe your ID."

I don't think I hear her correctly, but I reach for my ID and hand it to her. "I want to be an officer," I confide. "I hope this doesn't work against me."

She stares at me for a long time, her radio calling. My hand is extended, with the card still in it. She pushes it back toward me gently. "Ironic. Drive safe," she says. "If you can, consider turning around. It might be dangerous to be on the road right now." And with that, there is a wave of her burden passing between us.

I can't get regular radio, and I can't just listen to music. I need the news. I keep the static going until it slowly begins to clear up, and the reportage is vague. The focus is on the protesters, who have gotten violent, and merely listening to the story over satellite makes my stomach churn. Most of the original crowd being women and the counter-protesters being men, coverage picks up around the nation, then the world. "Women protesters get beat up by hordes of angry men." I turn the station.

"One woman couldn't take the abuse, and another went too far." I turn the station.

"The family is being questioned. They have a business that pokes fun at politics, but sources say that the eldest daughter is an extremist, part of the Antifa, and that her story of abuse is questionable, at best."

When I arrive, I climb the stairs and knock until my knuckles ache. My key doesn't work. An officer answers the door, and asks me who I am. I see his lips moving, and I can barely make out his business-like tone. My brothers sit with bleak expressions, and Allie is being questioned. We sit, unable to do anything, for hours, waiting to see if she'll be released. Joey says Allie was at the library most of the day, and there are witnesses to prove it. This is where she was picked up, after checking out myriad books on entrepreneurship. We are all asleep when she is escorted home.

"It's a war now," she says, nudging me. It's around 2 a.m. "They've been calling all day. My voicemail is full. I have interviews tomorrow. They want to speak with you, too."

"I'm so glad you're home."

"They have nothing on me, Molly May. You didn't doubt me, did you?"

"Hell no."

"So many people support me. But so many more people hate me," Allie whispers. My sister embraces me, and we begin to share a single thought, the way we used to as kids. *What next?*

I dial Rattle's number the next morning and hold the phone to my good ear. When he doesn't answer, I ask him to call me back if he's heard from Mom. Despite the number of people on this case, I can't help but entertain the idea that this is my problem to solve.

Despite all the noise in my ear, I have a foundation that allows me to think objectively, and while my brothers feign stoicism, I calm my sister the same way I used to calm Mom. "You need to understand the balance," I tell her before she makes another statement. "There are officers here helping. You need to be smart when you speak to the public. You have a platform now, and that can cause damage if you're not careful."

"I hear you, Molly May. I hear you."

We all wait to hear from Mom and never do. Joey's jeans are covered in something, and when I sit next to him, he becomes the little boy who ran to me when he saw something that scared him, the one who was afraid to go into dark places. He curls into my arms, and I tell him it will be okay. "I was screamed at," he says. "At the community center. I was performing, and someone ran up onstage and threw his drink at me."

"They're lashing out at me, at us, because they don't have a clear enemy," Allie says. She is pacing like an addict waiting for a fix, a creative soul waiting for an idea. "We just need to wait this out, unless she comes forward."

"Mom didn't do this," Myron says. "I don't know why you called Rattle. I don't know why you think that," he stammers, looking from me to Allie. My younger brother's eyes show something I've not seen before. They seem alive.

Allie glances out the window, where an officer is standing guard. The police are watching out for us, and I rush down the metal stairs to offer the man water or something to eat. He just nods. "This will all blow over. The public memory is short," he says.

"Thank you," I say. His name is Bradley, and he hands me his card.

The four of us kids, no longer kids, sit on the carpet of an apartment my mother secured with questionable funds, and Allie pulls out a notebook. She rips off a piece of paper and passes the notebook to me. I hand her a pen.

"Mom didn't do this," Myron says again as Allie begins to shuffle a deck of cards.

Months pass, and just as Officer Bradley said, people calm down, then they forget. They forget, that is, until the trial begins.

I arrive at the courthouse wearing a white top and black pants. A woman with dark hair and oversized sunglasses thinks I am a valet at the hotel next door, and she offers me her keys. I'm tempted to take them.

"I don't work here," I say, too loudly. She frowns.

"My mistake! But you don't have to yell at me, young lady."

"I'm pretty fucking deaf, so yes, yes I do," I say. As soon as the words leave my lips, I want to apologize; my annoyance shouldn't be directed at her. Vic wanted to come with me, and I told him no, but now I wish for his strength, the hand hold. I'm tempted to grab the hand of the woman who is now glowering at me. The world needs steadied.

When I arrive, I give my purse and earrings to a woman who runs them through a detector before handing them back. She directs me to the courtroom, and I walk without peripheral to the front row, where my brothers are sliding around in their seats. I nudge Joey, noticing his stubble. "You're such a man," I say, touching his chin.

"Ugh. Shhhh," he says, but his lips are pursing in a smile. I nod to Myron, who nods back. His cheeks are a healthy pink. Just as Allie told me, the boys are doing well. Maybe better than ever.

My sister doesn't look back. She sits, shoulders back, with monastic calm. Her hair is in a sleek bun, with a few curls hanging alongside her bangs. Her lips are pale, and her skin is paler than usual. Her eyes are fixed on the wall. "Please rise. The Court of the Second Judicial Circuit, Criminal Division, is now in session, the Honorable Judge John Creno presiding."

The judge invites the jury to sit, and I survey them. Mostly men. Numbness spreads throughout my stomach, up to my throat, as Griffin turns to look around the room. He is in a wheelchair, his eyes cloudy. We stare at each other a moment, and I remember him coming over just after my surgery—my sister's reaction then. He had tried to kill her, tried to silence her. I imagine I feel the same way Myron feels as he begins to stand. Joey uses all his strength to pull him back down. "No," I see him whisper, as though calling off a dog.

The pins, the nerves, the waiting. Then, the case is adjourned. To reconvene another day. I won't make the next hearing. Or the one after that. But my sister makes every single date, playing the long game, even at the expense of the business.

***

Timing is everything in this world. Though our mother was questioned, and each member of our family considered suspect over the years, no one is ever convicted of shooting Griffin. Meanwhile, two years after my sister's case against him was opened, then complicated by Griffin's injury, the judge rules in her favor. Like most such things, the impact is anticlimactic. We celebrate by meeting in the old neighborhood for pizza at what is now The Pizza Machine.

"A small win for the little guy," Allie says, lifting a greasy triangle of vegan cheese pizza to her lips.

"I knew you'd win. No enemy too big," I say, and I make a fist, curling it to my chest. She laughs and asks a kid in the next booth to take our picture holding our fists up, Rosie-style. It's an image that I'll later blow up and hang on my wall.

Not only is Griffin found guilty on all charges, but increased scrutiny into his past opens what seems an endless list of assaults, most of them sexual. Men and women begin coming forward with allegations against him, all thanks to my sister.

"You remember when Mom left?" Allie asks.

I nodded. "Well?"

"She said she would always take care of us."

I bite my bottom lip, surveying the pizza place. From my position in a torn booth, I can see our old home, the window I snuck out of to meet with Allie when we were kids, and everything felt like a movie to meet her.

"We're better off without her now," Allie says.

135

***

Not long after we celebrate, my sister begins getting phone calls, then more calls. Soon, her line is so congested that I can't get through. The public controversy reawakens on a larger scale, if only for a few days, and Allie is known as "the Midwestern woman who was assaulted by police." My sister's face is everywhere, which brings publicity, but it also brings harassment. She is assigned protection as protests break out.

I stand near Grandma Dee's couch, nibbling on bacon and watching as the camera zooms in dramatically on my sister's face. Allie's jaw is moving back and forth as though she is chewing on something, but I know she's not. It's her tell. She's irritated and holding back.

The morning-show host is treating her as a victim, and she is about to put him in his place. I square my shoulders as she squares hers. Sheroes. My sister smiles slowly, listening to the overly tanned man with the blond hair as he asks her how she has managed to live her life after being abused by a man who had taken an oath to protect and serve, after being defended by a mother who had no regard for human life.

"It's up to us to protect and serve," she says.

"Up to women?"

"Up to citizens who live in a police state. We must rise above the insidiousness that is a part of our society now. It begins with the government and trickles down to these few power-dizzy cops, but cops are also who kept me safe after the news broke."

The host looks away, reclaims his plastic smile.

"You suffered quite a few injuries, still as a child, and my notes say you didn't leave the house for almost a month after the attack. What gave you the strength to carry on?"

"My family," my sister says. "I learned what not to do from my family." She looks at the camera, as though searching for our mother.

My sister's eyes are intent and clear, and I close my eyes to imagine my mother watching. If she is, she's leaning back in her chair, drinking sparkling water out of a martini glass. Perhaps she's cleaning a gun and talking about Allie's *fucking bad taste* in clothes. *Who wears a T-shirt with a suit jacket*, she's likely saying to her boyfriend of the moment. But for all her leaning back and all her nonchalance, if Mom is watching, something inside her is softening as she hears the homage. It warms her.

My mother, who took on extra shifts and gigs, some less sensible than others, so that she could save enough to give us a fighting chance and left us to our own devices, is insane and driven and intolerant. She set us up, gave us opportunity. I think about Joshua and Rattle. I think about Rose — whose diabetes ate her checks as soon as they arrived in her account. I think about the packed pews at church, the tired and judgmental faces; the desire to feel a modicum of control.

My mother, who raised us to be intolerant in so many ways, caused us to be the opposite. In her way, she took control.

"I hope she's not watching, Molly May," Vic says. I feel his hand on my shoulder, and I place my hand over his. I open my eyes, catching the photo of my parents in my peripheral. If I ever have my own children, which I probably won't, I will try to remember Mom in a way that makes her feel accessible and earnest. Dad as the cool guy my sister likes to present him to be. I too will tell stories slant, but I already know that it will feel as though I am recalling episodes. Mom will soon join my father in this photo and become static and unreachable, a voice forever shouting in my deaf ear.

"There's no such thing as The Free," Allie tells the reporter. "We spend our lives fighting to get as close as we can to freedom, but we're all constrained by the biases of our parents, our predecessors. Maybe we haven't been ready for true freedom — we wouldn't know what to do with it. We need to listen to each other to make better decisions; then maybe we won't limit the next generation."

I stare at my sister now, a woman no longer defeated, despite messages of destruction and terror running along the banner below her. I close my eyes, my senses, and tell her I love her and that she's strong. We all are, but we have a lot to do. It's my turn. My stomach shifts, hard and heavy, and I open my eyes.

JASMINE

THE RIDE

Los Angeles, California – 2030

A woman in the lobby smells like synthetic oranges, which reminds me of summer in the Midwest. Summer in a place with seasons, not fires. I was fourteen years old when I first learned to drive. Sitting in Daddy's seat at the helm, I steered the wheel of his Volvo in circles around the vacant elementary school parking lot.

It was early on a Sunday morning, and the sun was just high enough to make me squint, likely forming my very first wrinkles. Damn wrinkles. It was July, and the car freshener claimed citrus, an unnatural orangey smell.

I remember his rare and fleeting patience that day as he instructed me to press lightly on the gas or ease into the brake, and how quickly that patience had faded when I closed my eyes and jerked the wheel away from the sun. He'd had to tug it the other way to right the car, and he screamed about his new tires as the smell of rubber overpowered the citrus.

I remember a low-pitch yell, and though I don't remember what I said back to him, the impact came immediately after. It was as though the words, any words, were a magnet for his fist. Dad hit me a lot, but this day my head smacked the inside of the car window hard enough that I began to think differently about the world.

"You have to play by the rules," his voice echoed. He continued to yell, even after checking the welt on the side of my forehead in a brief paternal flash. "You think you need to go to the fucking ER now?"

"No," I said. And as he nodded, I ran. I pushed the driver's side door open and jumped out of the car. I ran so quickly and with such agility, weaving around corners, dumpsters and cars, that I knew he'd never catch me. Someone honked when I decided to hide in the bus stop, and just when I was ready to steal away into the world, the real world beyond my sad little house on Green Street, a stray dog began to growl. It trapped me, as someone called, "Buses aren't running today," from the window. "She's over here, sir!"

The dog didn't budge; it felt as though the dog were my father's frontline, and I learned to hate dogs that day. Jumping up on the bus stop bench, I trembled, feeling for the round mass on my head, staring into the eyes that kept me from freedom.

There was no point in resisting when my father snatched me up and headed to the car, carrying me like a wet newspaper under his arm. I would come to understand his anger and disappointment when my own child would run away decades later, but I never hit her. I would never hit a child.

To be on one's own, unshackled by the intentional and unintentional abuses of those who are supposed to love and protect you, is to be pure and to fully feel the ground, the air, the solidity of the world. To face fears head-on. But I had cowered that day, whereas Allie did not, and I promised myself I never would again.

***

My mother would eat nectarines, and her breath always gave off the sour jolt of natural citrus, too, which made my throat close up when I was a kid. All I wanted was sweet then.

Brilliant at crosswords, Mom used to send in difficult puzzles for cash, and when I was old enough, I would help. The challenge of it was energizing, and the trivia seemed to help me in school, especially history. It helped me converse with adults, who seemed forever impressed by random facts, and dubious when the facts were new to them. I would feel a tingle in my belly as people would verify my claims and look impressed. "You have quite the genius on your hands," they'd say. I didn't need Google or Alexa. I had my mind.

My mother would nod and smile weakly, saying I must have gotten my brains from my father. Such bullshit. Mom had been a kind woman, but passive to a fault and all too willing to take a fist to the jaw—or head or chest or gut.

I see my mother sitting by the window with fading eyes. So passive that life itself beat her ass. She became anemic, and everything bruised her;

142

she became sicker and sicker, and died of a mysterious disease. I thought it weakness, pure weakness, a slow but early death invited.

What could be more depressing than reliving the past at the DMV?

I know to save these thoughts for therapy, which I blame for causing them to bubble to the surface in the first place. Too much self-reflection is the therapist's trick. They tap what shouldn't be tapped, and then you have to go back in time.

"What do you mean you're going to take my license?" a man hollers. His accent is Georgian, backwoods. I have a knack for placing regional accents and mimicking them.

"It's women who can't drive." He points back to me, which makes me smile ironically.

"Sir," the woman begins, rolling her eyes.

"No, hear me out. I make my claim based on real-life experience. I was following this one lady for almost thirty miles the other day. She had her turn signal on the whole time."

"Sir, this has nothing to do with—" the woman behind the counter begins to say. I walk toward them, intrigued.

He continues. "Thirty miles! When I finally caught up to her, I waved her over and said, 'Hey, baby girl, your left turn signal has been on for thirty miles.' And she just said, 'I know. That's where I hang my purse.' Moral of the story: women can't drive."

The man, wild-haired and thin, winks back at me, which I take as an invitation. I do my best version of his accent. "Well, now, mystery solved," I say. "I thought some creeper was following me the other day. Don't worry about how I drive my car." The woman behind the counter laughs now and leans in toward me.

"You want to stay up here at the counter? You can go next." There are at least twenty people before me, but I nod, sliding my number across the counter slyly.

"You from Georgia?" the man says, confused.

"Thomaston. Born and raised."

"Well, holy hell! That just dills my pickle."

"Don't come on to me now," I say with a smile. The man reminds me of Wile E. Coyote, the way he looks at me as though he needs a chase.

It has been years since I have been with a man, but this is most definitely not the one. I need to pass this driver's exam so I can get back on the road.

"What are you doing in Hollytown?" the man asks.

"Finding religion," I say, this being my go-to answer. He nods and is ushered off to the next station. I am tasked to look at a small house at the end of a target and identify flashes on the right and left that I do not see at all.

"Right, right, left," I say, guessing.

Joey could do impressions. My youngest. I imagine this man could be a muse for him. When I was still inside, Joey appeared on a reality TV show that was set up to allow young comics to compete, doing stand-up, and though he didn't place, the appearance got him attention. He began to get gigs. That kid was the only one to so much as write. His two long, diary-like letters gave me a little boost, I'll admit, but at the time I didn't think it was enough.

Allie couldn't reach out, of course not, but I expected to hear from Molly May, the sensitive one in the family. Joey wrote that she'd been accepted to the Academy and was "crushing it," as he put it. The girl who showed every emotion in the crunch of an eyebrow or tilt of her lips. I remember her watching cloudy, old *Police Academy* movies online; Joey doing impressions.

Molly May had chosen, as a young person, to take care of her grandmother and settle down. Who does that at the age of twenty in the modern world? There hadn't even been a war declared at the time, and she chose to protect and serve.

Then there was the child most like my own mother. Myron. Those sad eyes. He needed something to care about, that kid. I hope he found it.

I fight the urge to look him up, figure Molly May can fill me in when I arrive. Molly May can fill me in on everything. It's kind of funny that I never did time for shooting Griffin, but the credit cards I maxed out to set the kids up eventually caught up with me. So many credit cards, so much time. All the gigs in the world couldn't have set up a single mother of four the way she needed, to find freedom, so I had no choice. Who knows if the kids even talk about this, even care?

Allie is a commentator on a political news channel now, so she's hard to ignore. She is always in the news for saying what others are afraid to. Things that shatter a sheltered child's utopian view of the world. I must've done something right there; the girl's a survivor, and the man who attacked her has now paid on earth, as he will again.

A senior now, my ability to pass the visual test that qualifies me to drive seems a distant fantasy. The younger man, the Georgian, is still watching me, and I wink at him.

I don't see the lights or shapes at all, but I know the scale and have heard the letters being called for the last hour. A pattern is obvious; they change out the card three times, then begin again. If I get one wrong, I'll know. "C." I'm adept at reading micro-expressions and have learned to watch people's hands react to circumstance. With disappointment, there is a subtle tightening.

Ironic how things happen. I had been a matriarch in prison, but my kids seemed to thrive after I left. As much as they hurt me, this was also my plan. Selflessness is a dream, not a reality. These are the truths that come with age. When I get my picture taken for my license, I lay out the next steps. Rental car under a friend's name, pay up front, drive to Ohio, reconnect. I need to reconcile with my children.

If not reconcile, I want to shake the kids' hands and move on into the unknown for good. I want to hear what they're up to, really up to, and then journey around making ends meet as I always have. I have almost five hundred in product to sell, from lipsticks to body wash, and I've never been more on my game with the pitch. This is an honest living, the kind of gigs that could never have gotten me anywhere with four kids but can most definitely get me home to them. The goal is to unload it all by the time I get to Oklahoma.

"Hey there, silver princess," the wild-haired man says. "You like younger guys?"

"I do, but I don't have time for you," I say. I realize the accent has dropped and pick it back up. "I'm busier than a moth in a mitten."

"Ha! Here, give me a call sometime," he says, handing me his card. A truck driver.

"Where are you headed from here?" I ask, thinking this might be an opportunity.

"Arkansas, land of the blessed."

"When are you leaving?"

"Tomorrow. Staying at the Motel 6. Got a pretty little room."

**

Men are simple, but none are simpler than Mr. Bunt. He is from the Georgia sticks and just wants to talk all about fishing and family. All that man wants is company and a partner to trade jokes with on the road, and I choose to appease his desires. We are laughing, chatting about my four kids and his lack of any, when he begins to cry. "I always wanted a mini-me."

"Don't. I went to prison for my kids. They steal your life."

"Nothing worth stealing," he says. "What you think takes up all your precious time is what it's all about. That possum's on the stump."

I don't know how to interpret this phrase, so I tell him I need to get some shut-eye, and I lean back in the truck. People always want what they don't have.

Though he doesn't buy any product, thanks to Mr. Bunt, I am ahead of schedule when I get to Arkansas and am able to get a rental there without any trouble. I sell a lipstick to a woman who fills out my paperwork. Merry Berry Red, for the holidays.

What can I say? *I suppose I love you is a good place to start. I'll say, I don't know what all you want from me at this point, if anything. Probably you want me to leave you alone. But I did that time because I love you kids, and I'd kill for you. All life is a series of decisions, and I didn't know which one to make. I believe in you. I hope you know you're better than I am. I pause, wondering if this will come across in person.*

Maybe I should just leave the kids a note.

I pull off a long piece of a scratchy brown paper towel in the bathroom and sit on the toilet. "Dear kids, I hope you still do your dream boards. I prayed for an hour every day inside. Women are the worst prisoners, the worst, and I prayed to find equilibrium around those crazies. You know why women are the worst prisoners? Because they're not all victims, but people treat them like they are. Sure, we are in there for killing men who did something horrible, or trying to, or for trying to make ends meet in a world where society fucks us over, but we are no victims. And we have twice as much to prove. I could tell you stories. Maybe I will one day, and I'll tell you how much of me is in each of you. All I wanted was to get away. Do you understand that feeling yet?"

I realize I just wrote a memoir, so I crumple the letter and throw it in the toilet. It refuses to go down with a flush. I write three goals on another piece of towel: 1. Find my kids. 2. Find Blake and apologize. 3. Release.

I clasp my hands together, balancing a giant key on my right thigh, and ignore the sour scent and pounding knock. For the first time in a long time, I close my eyes and see that silly bald man who told me what I knew, and I feel a heat rise in my belly.

"Hurry the fuck up," a woman's voice calls. "It's snowing like a motherfucker out here." I breathe deeply, staring through half-closed eyes at a crack in the pale green tile in front of me.

Molly May will be the bridge to the rest of my kids, I know it. The thought of her face, so round and kind, stops my breath. I need to reorient, as Dr. Alien suggests each time I speak about my children and the blankness takes over. "We all have different values," my new friend said. Maybe. Or maybe we just think we do.

Another knock arrives, a different cadence, and when I open the door, a teenager pushes past me and rushes to the toilet without closing the door. I hand her the key.

There are over 10,000 gas stations in the States, and most are independently run. California uses more gas than any other state, but the state also houses more alternative fuel vehicles. The apple blossom is the official state flower of Arkansas. The teenager who pushed past was no doubt a Taurus. My mind hums.

"Such a genius," people used to say. They didn't understand that my mind simply wouldn't slow down.

I rev up my hybrid rental and navigate the snow. The average snowfall in Arkansas is something I don't know, but I assume it's not more than a few inches.

Mr. Bunt texts me as I drive. "Hey, baby girl. Thanks for the company. I'll meet you on the other side."

"Till then," I type, thinking about all I've been through. The pain, the curse, the loss of a husband, and it all becomes a bit of a whirlwind that blinds me like the light in front of me, which has turned red. I skid, and the sun catches my eye. Like clockwork, I am back in the car, and I jerk the wheel the opposite way my father had instructed me to, coming to a sloppy stop on a patch of ice.

I look around to discover that no one else is on the road. The sun is cutting across a field nearby, and I notice the gold-laced frosted expanse growing fuzzy. It seems to go on forever. I attempt to roll my neck and realize that it won't move. With the subtle scent of citrus wafting in the air, I call on all my strength to reach for the pen and notebook resting on the passenger's seat. Yes, a note might be best.

MOLLY MAY

THE FREE
Toledo, Ohio – 2030

For a long time, I knew Mom was in prison in California. I looked her up regularly in CDCR. Imagining her the matriarch, the one who "ran shit" inside, I fought the urge to call over and have someone check up on her. She'd been convicted of identity fraud and petty theft. She stole the Toledo surgeon's identity, among quite a few others, and had paid our rent those months on cash advances from accounts she'd tapped. I suspected that she had padded Grandma Dee's accounts as well, but I had no way of knowing how much money was in her accounts before I took them over.

According to Mom's file, she hadn't been on good behavior since she'd been inside either. She was suspected of starting a cult. She'd been in fights, but mostly in the first few years. I'd expected she'd be released early, but whenever I checked in, she was still there.

The nice cars, nice clothes before she left us ... I imagine the entitlement she always felt, despite not having much, and I wonder if she feels regret. Likely not. It went on like this for years; then the day came.

"Who is that?" Annette, an administrator in my department, asked before Happy Hour one Friday. I didn't look around. The day had come, and Mom's pre-release process was finally in place, and she was set to meet with a psychologist. "I've seen you look her up before."

I shrugged as my mother's eyes, wandering even in the steadiness of a photo, held me. Annette evaluated her image, then nodded at me with either knowing or resignation; I'm not sure which. As my coworker walked off, I closed the window for the last time.

I imagined Mom the matriarch for a long time because I couldn't allow myself to think any other way. I couldn't accept what I was beginning to know—how fragile she was. When I saw that she was released, I planned to reach out. I had the resources to find her, after all, but I kept putting it off. I mean, why find someone who doesn't want to be found?

Joey and I spoke on the phone regularly, and he'd mentioned writing to her while she was inside, said that she never wrote back. I figured the same would happen to me, and I refused to be abandoned again.

***

It's 2 p.m. on a Thursday, a few days before Christmas and near the anniversary of my father's death. I'm dusting the ornaments on Grandma Dee's tree, readying them for the actual season. As the teeth-grating (and soon-to-be-replaced) doorbell sounds, I wonder briefly if it's her. Once the door is open and my eyes settle on a pair of freshly ironed pants, I know what I am about to hear.

The person at the door speaks slowly, with soft eyes. I do not know if I say anything in return. Even seconds after the door closes, I can only remember the details of what she said and the way her face moved, as though in slow motion.

It could have been her at the door. My mother had been trying to get home when she hit black ice in Indiana and ended up in a ditch, her rental positioned nose-down, the driver's-side door jammed. Her head hit hard, and she must've known it. I have a notebook in my hand that contains a letter. She was headed toward us.

I hold the notebook tight, struck numb and dumb by shock, and I close my eyes, imagining her behind me.

"Hon?" Vic says. He guides me toward the kitchen table, where we once did resolutions and ate pie as kids, looking at our mother as though she were otherworldly, Allie and I trading glances of desperation or anger or resolve.

"She's gone," I say, and I don't hear my own words. My hearing is no better, only slightly worse, as doctors predicted, but I temporarily lose my voice.

The notebook Mom left behind is small and full of jagged script. She wrote us a letter, seemingly aware that no one would be able to stop by the side of the road and help her in time. At the top, barely readable, is a command: *Whoever finds this, give it to Molly May.* Below this line, even less legible script: *You don't hear, so you listen best. Therapy helped me to see. It helped me to see that I lost my way...*

      I stop reading and yell for Vic, who is helping Grandma Dee walk to the kitchen, so that I can tell her. I ask him to read the note to the end. "Is it safe?" I ask. I want to tell him to hurry up as he reads. I watch as his eyebrows crinkle. He holds the notebook at angles, as though trying to decipher the script.

      "It's safe," he says. I've done this for him, throughout his divorce, reading endless bad news and odd messaging, dulling the edges of words. I'm tempted to tear the letter apart, to summarize the message and destroy the feeling of her body hovering behind me, glaring down at whatever I am doing wrong. Instead, I call on my siblings, and they agree to come to me. I tell Grandma Dee, who is fully senile now, and she simply nods.

      "With the angels," she says.

***

      In her will, Mom requests to be buried next to our father in Toledo, a plot that has already been promised to another family. She wants to have Madonna playing during her funeral, along with a playlist of '90s hits, and the list of guest names she leaves me to contact includes people I've never met, from her life before children, and people I worry may not exist, like a person named Dr. Alien.

      I am to contact women whose names have changed and men who have likely passed away. And I call them all. I do everything she knew I would do, and it dawns on me that though this whole time I've looked to my sister for the answers, Mom knew I was strong enough to handle it. The funeral of a woman who spent the better part of her last decades in prison is not a large funeral. But it will be revelatory.

      I want your sister to speak.

***

      When my brothers arrive, the three of us play board games to pass the time. Joey annihilates in *Scattergories* as we wait for Allie, whose plane was delayed in Dallas. Grandma, who sleeps most of the day now, hums along to "Hallelujah." Vic makes French toast, and we all drink more coffee than we should. Speeding things up has always settled our family down.

      "She wants me to wait till you are all here to read this," I tell them, waving Mom's notebook gently. It's strange to have her here in the room

153

again, just as distant.

"That's her now," Joey says, motioning to the notebook. He's a man now, and I can't help but think about his scrawny younger self teetering around the house, doing impressions of Johnny Depp. Myron, who found love at a yoga studio, of all places, sits cross-legged next to Joey, serene as a statue.

I was so wrong about so much. Mom was so wrong about so much.

When Allie arrives, it's almost midnight. Joey and I are drinking white wine, reminiscing about old dances we'd do in the living room when Mom wasn't around to scold us. My brothers are laughing as I attempt to re-create a dance move Joey used to do in which he'd knock his knees together rapidly. Vic shakes his head, unable to grasp our humor, which makes me appreciate him even more. He still runs the café, and he's likely exhausted, irritated that Allie is taking so long to arrive. She's sent delay after delay notice. I am about to tell him that we might as well turn in for the night, when the door opens. No knock, no buzz.

Allie arrives starched and prim, a talking head with plastic-like hair. I touch it to make sure it's real. Her makeup is pristine, almost overdone. She is all newscaster glam, and I tell her that I worry she may have turned to paraffin wax; she smiles and takes her hair out of a chignon.

"It's so good to be home," she says, kicking off her heels and giving us each a hug. "I miss her."

None of us speak. My sister kisses everyone, wandering around and looking behind and beneath items. Grandma Dee is asleep, so she whispers. "I'm so proud of you both," Allie says to my brothers, looking from one to another. Her eyes settle on Myron, who scratches his soon-to-be-bald head. "What yoga move will cure this back pain? I was stuffed into a middle seat for the last four hours," she says.

Myron just stares at her a moment, then tells her to straighten her spine and circle her arms down, around, and up. He shows her a twist that Joey joins in on, but Allie quickly abandons the idea, leaving my stoic brother to roll his eyes. I watch Allie, try to will her to stop moving, but she is too keyed up. She rushes to the kitchen to get a cup of coffee, but we do not have any made, then comes back and continues examining the house, tracing the walls and repositioning knickknacks.

"It looks good in here."

We've redecorated considerably, replacing the outdated furniture and repainting the walls in bolder, deeper tones. Apart from Grandma's old tree and that ear-grating buzzer, the house has undergone generational and sensorial shifts. It is all warm colors now, all invitation.

There are no words for the tangle of emotions I feel as my sister's eyes land on my service awards. My special commendation ribbons are framed above the fireplace. My criminal justice diploma is propped up next to the photo of our parents. A copy of one of Mom's fraudulent accounts is tucked into the back of the frame. For a while, I kept all the evidence of her crimes, petty and not so much, as a reminder.

Vic hands Allie a Unity Coffee mug, and she thanks him, staring at the logo as she finally takes a seat. Vic is getting texts from the business now, a new employee who has been nothing but trouble. Life goes on. "I'm sorry, guys. One minute," he says, excusing himself to return a call. I hear him say, "family emergency," and get a chill.

Before I know it, Allie's up and wandering around again. I can hear her sneaking up on me. Tackle-hugging me like she used to when I was a little kid, she whispers to me, "I'm so proud of you, too. We're doing the work." I can hear the wind outside, and the heavy breathing of our vents circulating dry, warm air. I stare at my sister's eyes, willing them to stop moving. I see my mother's energy raging inside of her, unresolved, and I want to help.

***

Settling down, playing games, we ready ourselves, pretending that we don't have to plan and discuss the funeral. We'll do all that tomorrow. Today, we say goodbye to Mom and hello to the scattershot family we've become. Mid-triple-letter score, I am about to gloat when Grandma Dee wakes with a chuckle, as she often does.

She rarely moves from her recliner or the couch after 5 p.m., and she's been dozing off and waking up with the noise. Her constant state of peace and sweet interjections are things I've come to believe will last forever.

"Come on, Jasmine. I'm knitting," she says to my sister, and Allie responds with a bittersweet smile. Now that Grandma is awake, my mother's words refuse to wait. We sit around at attention, and after

I make Joey record my score, as Grandma Dee hums mindlessly in the background and picks up a knitting project—an endless green scarf for a son she no longer knows is gone—I ready myself to read Mom's words.

She speaks to us, and I am her voice. I look back to find Vic in the kitchen making coffee. Our pup, a boxer-mix we rescued, is leaning against his leg. I click my tongue to the roof of my mouth, and Lucky bounds my way. I scratch below his chin as I continue.

I've had a lot of diagnosis, kids. A bald man told me to put oil on my heels every night for 40 days. I had reiki and tried diets and meditation and so many gods. So many gods, kids. I understand now, but I'm dying. No one's going to come out here and find me, and I hope I can write enough here to say what I want ...

You didn't need me, and I'm glad. I want you to know that I'm glad. I'm sure you are all happier now. If you aren't, you will be. Just wait. There are places in the world, you know, where you can walk into any coffee shop and know that the person you are speaking with is a millionaire. I wanted to get to one of those places. I thought if I had enough money—freedom—I'd find peace. I have these shifts. This energy that I can't seem to release.

I pause, wanting to stretch out each word, reaching for the warm mug beside me, the mint tea releasing soft steam, and I hold it in both hands a moment; the notebook feels heavy in my lap. I look up at my brothers, but they just look down. I continue.

You all are better than me. The swell and salt fill my eyes. *You all are better equipped. You are whole.* I hand the letter to Allie.

"I got this," she says. She stretches back, tracing the text I read before continuing.

There were a lot of women in that prison. Mothers. This country imprisons more women than any other country in the world, and my new psychologist told me that most have a mental illness. I tell you this so you are mindful, Molly May. All of you.

I know a lot about your lives post-me. I've been keeping tabs, but I know better than to interfere. Dr. A diagnosed me as having a borderline personality, for what it's worth. Diagnoses don't matter, but there it is. The shifts.

We all have shit to deal with.

Keep each other safe. Myron, Allie, Molly May, I won't be sneaking up on you anymore. Joey, keep my legacy alive. Allie, you're whole, kiddo. Full to the brim.

Joey's face turns gray. Allie nods knowingly.

Your father and I did a few things right. Know that we tried. We were normal people for a time. We had other places to go, he and I. Not better, just other. I'll meet Jackson soon. We have a lot to dis—

"That's it," Allie says. It's illegible. We pass the letter off, huddling over the last line, so thick it looks as though she went over it twice. Joey reads it. *The moments* ... "It's all I can make out."

Glancing over at the photograph of my parents, I feel a hand on my shoulder. I cover the warmth with my own and close my eyes.

"I remember it," Allie says. "I remember her before, when she was different. The moments. She was ... I don't know. Happy. Herself. *Free.* I always remembered, and that's why I couldn't stand who she became. She was trying to fight it."

"I saw moments," I say.

Joey stands. "I saw moments, too."

"Mom was fierce," Myron says. "She didn't want to be a mother, but she did the best she could."

"Bullshit," Grandma Dee says. She looks over at the image and adds, "Those two were in love. They wanted you." She places her scarf on her lap, and I stand and reposition a blanket around her shoulders as her eyes close. She continues to speak, a smile spreading across her lips. "You think people who aren't willing would have so many kids?" She gestures at the four of us, pausing her finger on each one.

"Good point," Myron says. He looks to Joey. "It's funny that she called you out about your show. You think she's been watching all of us like that?"

"Without a doubt," Allie says.

Without hesitating, my youngest brother assumes his role. "This one's for Mom, who finally found her *Self* in prison."

Vic takes my seat on the couch, and I squeeze in beside him. "You have a great family," he tells me, as my brother acts out entire scenes from *The Wizard of Oz*, a classic in our living room as kids. Allie laughs loud and large beside him.

"I'm proud of that, too," Allie whispers to me between gales of laughter, gesturing to a plaque on the wall. "You listened to yourself."

"These are the moments we fight for," I tell her.

Just like that, time bends, and I can see the curious kids we once were, replete with goofy innocence, the rift yet to begin. I don't know what shifts in people to make them think they need to get away, but Mom tried, and I don't need to understand her.

As I absorb my siblings' laughter, throaty and loud, the world feels crisp and alive. Memories once closed off return. I trace the notebook page, and I can feel myself out of breath as I run. I see my sister running around at the park, Mom and Dad yelling after us to make sure we stay in view. I see us attempting to break free, even then, hiding behind bushes or skirting the edge of the playground—going a little farther than allowed.

As the scenes come to life in my mind, time and loss no longer matter. The threatening scenes, the guns, the rage. I wonder briefly if I am making it all up.

I can access some version of the past beyond the split. I can see my parents before their light faded. I could speculate as to why they struggled, but I've been trying to do that my entire life. Now, I see the sacrifice. I see the moments.

Mom is pregnant. She pushes Allie and me on the swings, her palms flat and warm against our backs, enabling us to fly. In this moment, she is whole, the way I imagine she was at the end of her journey. Dad watches through a camera lens and waves, and he is familiar. They trade odd facts and laugh at things no one else would. Allie ruffles my hair and looks back at Mom; they share a lifetime in that single gaze.

We are all together again in my mind, content and absolute, fixed in time but forever free. This moment is all I need. My sister snuggles up next to me and leans in, resting her head on my shoulder, and together we are unshakable. Solid and free, ready to take on the world.

ACKNOWLEDGMENTS

Excerpts from this novel-in-stories have been included in *Fairlight Books*, *Atticus Review*, *Juked*, and *Little Fictions*. The chapter "Nothing Wrong" was one of two finalists in *Columbia Journal*'s Winter Contest for Fiction, and a portion of the manuscript, "Lost Her Way," was shortlisted for the 2017 Book Pipeline Competition.

CPSIA information can be obtained
at www.ICGtesting.com
Printed in the USA
LVHW090409230620
658770LV00002B/385

9 781733 089876